THE PRICE OF FREEDOM

When his wife is murdered, the victim of an assassin's bullet, businessman Dell Weston soon finds his life is falling apart. Betrayed by his partner, he loses control of his company, and descends into the lower strata of a dog-eat-dog society. Somehow, Dell manages to survive long enough to question the very fabric of civilisation — and the role played by the mysterious figures in grey — the Arbitrators . . .

Books by E. C. Tubb
in the Linford Mystery Library:

ASSIGNMENT NEW YORK
THE POSSESSED
THE LIFE BUYER
DEAD WEIGHT
DEATH IS A DREAM
MOON BASE
FEAR OF STRANGERS
TIDE OF DEATH
FOOTSTEPS OF ANGELS
THE SPACE-BORN
SECRET OF THE TOWERS

Established in 1972 to provide funds for research, diagnosis and treatment of eye diseases. Examples of contributions made are: —

A Children's Assessment Unit at Moorfield's Hospital, London.

•

Twin operating theatres at the Western Ophthalmic Hospital, London.

•

A Chair of Ophthalmology at the Royal Australian College of Ophthalmologists.

•

The Ulverscroft Children's Eye Unit at the Great Ormond Street Hospital For Sick Children, London.

You can help further the work of the Foundation by making a donation or leaving a legacy. Every contribution, no matter how small, is received with gratitude. Please write for details to:

THE ULVERSCROFT FOUNDATION,
The Green, Bradgate Road, Anstey,
Leicester LE7 7FU, England.
Telephone: (0116) 236 4325

In Australia write to:
THE ULVERSCROFT FOUNDATION,
c/o The Royal Australian and New Zealand
College of Ophthalmologists,
94-98 Chalmers Street, Surry Hills,
N.S.W. 2010, Australia

E. C. TUBB

THE PRICE OF FREEDOM

Complete and Unabridged

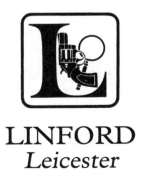

LINFORD
Leicester

First published in Great Britain

First Linford Edition
published 2008

Copyright © 1953 by E. C. Tubb

British Library CIP Data

Tubb, E. C.
  The price of freedom.—Large print ed.—
Linford mystery library
1. Detective and mystery stories
2. Large type books
I. Title
823.9'14 [F]

ISBN 978–1–84782–373–1

Published by
F. A. Thorpe (Publishing)
Anstey, Leicestershire

Set by Words & Graphics Ltd.
Anstey, Leicestershire
Printed and bound in Great Britain by
T. J. International Ltd., Padstow, Cornwall

This book is printed on acid-free paper

1

He awoke to the thin sound of shots and for a moment lay silent in the darkness, ears strained and nerves tense as he listened to the brittle sounds from the street below. Footsteps raced along the concrete of the pavement. Others thudded heavily behind them and a shouted warning echoed from the shuttered windows and smooth face of the building. A gun snapped angrily, glass shattered, and a man screamed in pain and terror. More shots, then silence, and the warm, soft darkness of sleep coiled temptingly around him.

He thrust it aside, forcing himself away and shivering a little in the pre-dawn chill. Carefully he reached for slippers and a robe, fumbling in the darkness and cursing softly as a chair fell with a crash. Lights flashed and a woman blinked sleepily at him from the second of twin beds.

'Dell, what on Earth are you doing?'

'Sorry, Madge.' He rubbed a bruised shin and narrowed his eyes against the too-bright glare. 'Someone was shooting in the streets and the noise woke me up.'

'Go back to sleep then.' Cat-like she turned and buried her face in the soft pillow.

'But it could be serious.'

'What of it?' Irritably she twisted on the bed, her eyes closed against the lights. 'The Guards will handle it. Turn off the lights and get back into bed.'

He hesitated, drawing the robe more tightly around him as his body lost the warmth of sleep. He stepped towards the window, one hand half raised as if to twitch aside the curtain, then stopped at the sound of his wife's harsh voice.

'Dell! Are you mad? What do you think you are doing now?'

'I wondered if I could see anything?' He flushed a little beneath her look of undisguised contempt. 'Someone might be hurt.'

'Sometimes I wonder why I ever had to marry such a fool,' she snapped acidly. 'It isn't enough that you have to be a moralist, a laughing stock among the other business men, you have to expose us both to danger as well. How do you know that someone isn't out there just waiting to shoot you dead?'

'Why should there be?'

'How should I know? You're a business-man aren't you?' Irritably she reached for a short fur jacket and pulled it around her too-plump shoulders. Sitting up in bed she lit a cigarette and blew thick streamers of smoke towards the fluores-cents, the dimmed light gleaming from the artificial blondness of her hair.

'Now that you've managed to spoil my sleep,' she grumbled, 'you may as well make some coffee. At least that would be useful.'

While he waited for the percolator to boil he stared at his reflection in the kitchen mirror and frowned at the growing lines of tiredness and worry. Still nearer thirty than forty, yet his thick, dark hair showed traces of grey at the temples, and premature age had placed its mark around eyes and mouth.

Worry, he thought. Worry and the

constant necessity of making more and more money. A too-young marriage to a too-greedy wife. A business which could be profitable but which his own stupid morals forced to run at a starvation margin of profit, and the steady pressure of a money-hungry partner clashing with his own innate convictions.

Bender was right, of course. Bender was always right. There was no reason why the business shouldn't provide more than enough for the both of them, no reason but his own conscience and the stubborn morality that made him a figure of fun and derision in business circles. Madge knew it, and never ceased telling him just what she thought about it. One day she would leave him, and somehow he just couldn't worry about that probability.

The hissing of the percolator jerked him from his mood of self-pity. He wrinkled his nose at the sickly smell of marijuana coiling about the bedroom, and set down the coffee tray with a clatter of cups. 'Do you have to smoke that stuff?'

'Why shouldn't I?' Madge glared at him from the bed and deliberately blew smoke into his face. 'All the other girls at the club do, their husbands too. You'd be a lot better if you had a smoke now and again.'

'I do smoke,' he corrected.

'Tobacco,' she sneered. 'Sissy stuff.' She dragged deeper on her cigarette. 'That's the trouble with all you moralists — because you don't want to do a thing, it must be wrong. You, and people like you made the world what it was. Prigs! Sissy cowards! Weaklings! You just haven't got the guts to be a man.'

'If by that you mean I don't dope myself senseless, drink myself blind, beat my wife, chase women and shoot unarmed men, then you're right. If that's being a man then I want no part of it.'

'And who do you think wants any part of you?'

'You did — once.'

'Once was a long time ago,' she sneered. 'I've grown up since then. I've learned what money can do, and what life should be like. If you didn't have money things might be different, but you're a potential millionaire and you owe it to me to cash in on the demand.'

'No!'

'Why not?'

'I'd rather not talk about it, not now. Have some more coffee then let's get back to sleep. I'm tired.'

'Tired? You're always tired. I'm tired too, tired of a husband who is only half a man. A lousy stinking moralist, a coward. Why can't you be like Bender? Why did I ever marry you?'

'Because you were a lazy slut hungry for a meal ticket. That's why. What have you to offer a man? Look at you! Drugged, half insane, greedy, too lazy even to take a bath.'

'You — !' He ducked as the coffee cup swung towards his head, the fragile china shattering on the wall behind.

He winced at the stream of abuse pouring from her twisting lips, and with a quick, smooth motion, gripped her wrists and squeezed — hard.

'Shut up,' he said without anger. 'If you want to leave me you know where the door is and I promise that I won't try to stop you.'

'You'd like that wouldn't you? You'd like to get rid of me, but I'm not going, do you hear? I'm not going!' She smiled, suddenly calm, the thick white flesh of her features creasing into ugly folds. 'If you want to get rid of me so much, then why not do it the right way?'

'What are you talking about?'

'You know what I mean! If you were a man at all you'd have offered it to me before. One half of all you own. I'm your wife, aren't I? I'm entitled to it by Ethical Contract and believe me I'm going to see that I get it.'

'I could kick you out without a penny,' he said coldly. 'We've no children and I have no moral obligation to you. If I wished, you'd be out on the street tomorrow.'

'And you'd be dead the day after!'

In the sudden silence the hum from the air-conditioner echoed startlingly loud. He stood and looked down at her slowly releasing his grasp on her wrists. Automatically she began to rub the red marks where his fingers had gripped.

'What did you say?' The menace in his voice sent her recoiling away from him, the sheets twisting round her legs.

'Don't touch me! If you hurt me you'll be sorry, I . . . ' She stopped, one hand pressed against her mouth, her eyes suddenly wide and frightened.

'So it's true,' he said grimly. 'You've joined a Bunco Group.'

'No, Dell. No, I promise you! Some of the girls were talking down at the club, it seemed a good idea. Don't look at me like that, Dell! I didn't join, I didn't!'

'But you thought about it,' he snapped. 'God! What did I ever see in you?' Disgustedly he turned away and mechanically picked up the pieces of the broken cup. The videophone shrilled its attention signal as he straightened and impatiently he closed the circuit.

The screen flared then steadied into flickering brilliance and the hard young face of his partner stared at him from the framed plastic.

'Dell,' he said excitedly. 'There has been trouble at the factory. McKeefe called to say that there had been a raid.'

'Again?' Dell tried not to feel the growing ball of sickness in the pit of his stomach. 'Did they get anything?'

'No. McKeefe's guards caught them in time. Three dead, and none of our guards injured.'

'Good. Any idea who it was?'

Bender shrugged, his cynical eyes glittering from the reflected transmission lights. 'I told you that the cartel intended to apply pressure. Maybe it's their way of giving a hint.'

'I doubt that. The Contract would stop them doing anything which could recoil on them, if they were caught the other groups would crucify them.'

'What other groups?' Bender laughed without humour. 'You're too trusting, Dell. I meant to have a talk with you soon, it had better be this morning when you arrive. Unless you can be made to see reason, we'll both be out of business.'

'Are you going down to the factory now?'

'Are you serious?' Bender stared from the screen, then smiled contemptuously.

'Get wise to yourself, Dell. The way you've been handling the business makes us both marked men. I'll see you tomorrow.'

He gestured, and stepped back from the darkening screen. Tiredly. Dell opened the circuit and crossed the room. Madge looked up from where she sat half crouched amid the tangled sheets. She had lit another cigarette, and from the unnatural glitter of her eyes, Dell knew that the drug was beginning to take effect.

'What did he want?'

'Trouble down at the factory. Someone tried a raid.'

'Serves you right,' she snapped brutally. 'If you only did what you should do, there'd be no more raids.' She squinted through the sickly smoke. 'After all you can't blame them.'

'Don't let's go over all that again now,' he said irritably. 'I've enough to worry about as it is.' He poured coffee, and grimaced at the almost cold liquid. 'Like some more to drink?'

'May as well, there's nothing else to do is there?'

'Not much,' he said drily, 'but that's a matter of opinion.'

Back in the kitchen he rinsed his mouth and washed his face and hands. His eyes felt gritty, overtired and with the sand of lost sleep grinding beneath his puffed lids. The percolator boiled, and he poured two cups of fragrant coffee. Going to a wall cabinet he fumbled among the nest of bottles until he found a small phial containing little white tablets. He dropped one into each cup watching the slight effervescence rise and die, and then spilled a second into his wife's cup. The way he felt he was in no mood to combat the maudlin affection that was the inevitable effect of marijuana on his wife.

The thick, sickly scent of the smouldering hemp hung heavily in the bedroom, and setting down the cups he moved towards the window. Madge watched him wide-eyed.

'Dell! Don't do it, Dell!'

'We've got to have some air in here,' he snapped. 'Stop worrying, nobody's going to kill me.'

He twitched aside the curtain, and

heard the thud of his wife's bare feet as she left the bed and crossed the room towards him.

'Dell!'

'Stop it!' He shrugged aside her hand, and threw open the window.

For a moment he stood there, breathing deep of the chill night air, feeling his lungs expand as he drew in the clean, moist breeze. Curiously he stared down at the deserted street, but could see no signs of the conflict that had woken him. He smiled as he felt the cool wind move gently against his flushed features, and tried not to be irritated at the touch of his wife's plump hands as she tried to draw him away from the window.

Something hit the glass with a sharp click. Something seared his ear with the sound of an angry bee. From a shadowy shape on the roof opposite a finger of flame stabbed at him, and the sharp snap of a high velocity rifle echoed from the building.

Desperately he threw himself back into the room, twisting away from the window, and rolling across the floor.

'The lights, Madge! Cut the lights!'

The fluorescents still blazed, and snarling with impatience Dell threw himself towards the switch. Darkness closed over the room, and frantically he pressed the alarm stud.

'Yes?' The voice was metallic and devoid of emotion.

'Assassins on the roof opposite. Room seventy-four here. Dell Watson. They fired three shots at me.'

'Right.'

From the roof floodlights blazed, turning the night into brilliant day. They swept across the deserted street, the face of the building opposite, the roof. A machine-gun chattered a harsh warning, then fell silent. The lights died, the noise, darkness returned shielding everything with its soft embrace.

Dell sagged against the wall feeling the weakness of reaction from immediate danger. Something trickled down the side of his face, and when he touched it, his fingers came away wet and warm. The doorbell uttered its low hum.

The house guard was hard, young and

very efficient. He carried a handbeam, and by its light he closed the proofed window and drew the curtains.

'You may put on the lights now, sir.'

The fluorescents blazed into sudden light, and Dell blinked painfully in the harsh glare, staring stupidly at the red stains on his fingers.

'They tried to kill me,' he muttered. 'They tried to kill me.'

'Are you seriously injured, sir. Shall I call the hospital?'

'No, it's just a scratch.' He looked at the guard. 'Did you get whoever it was?'

'No. They had too great a start, but we have warned all the business section.' He stared curiously at the prostrate figure of Madge. 'Your wife, sir?'

'Fainted, I suppose.' Dell crossed the room and stooped over the untidy heap of white flesh and flimsy night attire. He touched one shoulder and shook it urgently. 'Madge! Get up, Madge! It's all over now. Madge!'

He knew even before he saw the widening stain of seeping red. He could tell by the coldness of the shoulder, by the pitiful broken appearance of what had once been a living creature. She was dead, her chest smashed by an assassin's bullet, the red blood of her life an ugly splotch on the pale blue of the carpet.

He was surprised to find that he was crying.

2

Dawn came with a mist of rain and a bitter warning of near winter. A cold grey light began to fill the room and the hard sounds of scurrying footsteps echoed faintly from the filling streets. A strato-liner passed overhead with a high-pitched whistle of jets, and for a moment the proofed glass of the windows quivered in sympathy to the sound. It passed, and in the following silence the little everyday noises seemed strangely loud.

Dell stood, still dressed in his robe and slippers, and stared at the ugly splotch on the pale blue of the carpet. He felt numb, as if all emotion had been drained away leaving but the shell of a man. He hadn't loved his wife, hadn't loved her for too long, but it was a terrible thing to see a woman killed by the smashing impact of an assassin's bullet. It was a terrible thing to see someone you had once loved and cared for, had shared life with for over ten years, lying dead at your feet.

He looked up at the harsh sound of a forcibly cleared throat, and tried to forget his grief.

Captain Hanson, the house guard, shifted the weapon at his belt, and tried to look sympathetic. He failed. Sympathy to him was an alien emotion, he had seen too much death, too much pain and suffering to be anything but cynical.

'If you would just let me have a few details, sir,' he said. 'You gave the alarm at five-thirty, is that correct?'

'Yes.'

'Did the response satisfy you?'

'Yes.' Dell passed a hand wearily through his rumpled hair. 'I'm not blaming the guards. The assassin had already fired when I gave the alarm.'

'I see.' Hanson frowned, looking at the carpet, he didn't seem to notice the ugly stain. 'Are you complaining of any laxity on the part of the house guard, sir?'

'No.'

'Good.' The captain looked relieved. 'You know how it is these days, no matter how we try, how good our record,

17

someone has only to whisper a few insinuations and our contract gets revoked.' He slipped a few papers from a briefcase resting on the floor beside him. 'As far as I can make out, you opened the window, leaned out for a breath of air and the assassin fired at you from the roof of the building opposite. Is that correct?'

'Yes.'

'But you did open the window?'

'I told you that I did, what more do you want?'

'Nothing, sir. Nothing. The blame obviously rests with the house guard of the other building.' The captain tried not to show his satisfaction, he was far too well mannered to give voice to his conviction that any man fool enough to target himself against an open, lighted window at night deserved all he got.

'Is that all?'

'Yes, sir.' Hanson signed and thumb-printed an official looking document, and held out another for Dell's attention.

'If you will just sign and mark this clearance, sir? It absolves us from all blame, and you may rely on me to see that the house guard on the other building is changed within twenty-four hours.'

'I see, and I suppose that you will take over the contract.'

'Naturally, sir. Thank you. Here is my sworn deposition as to the manner of your wife's death. I'll send a copy to the central records as usual.'

Dell stared at the thin sheet of white paper, and frowned at the guard.

'Do I need this?'

'It may be advisable, sir.'

'You mean that a Bunco Group may think that I killed her myself?'

'Hardly, sir, but it would be wise to take precautions.'

'Madge wouldn't have done that.'

'No, sir.'

'She wouldn't have joined such a group, she told me herself.'

'Of course not, sir, but . . . ?' Hanson dropped the paper on to a low table. 'Shall I make arrangements for the cremation, sir?'

'Yes. Yes, do as you like, but get out now. Get out!'

The door closed softly behind the broad figure of the guard, and bitterly Dell stared al the mocking whiteness of the paper. Hanson was right of course. He couldn't be sure that Madge hadn't joined a Bunco Group. If they blamed him for her death, then by the terms of their contract they were bound to hunt him down like a mad dog. It was sheer common sense to advertise the deposition; he couldn't be blamed for accidents or the actions of others. Irritably he headed for the shower.

The hot water washed some of the numb ache from his bones, and relaxed his nerves a little. Carefully he shaved and dressed, wrapping the scarlet sash around the waist of green trousers and yellow blouse. Knee boots of yellow leather and a short jacket of green completed his attire and as protection against the cold rain he wrapped a cloak of vivid emerald around his shoulders. When he was dressed he pressed the intercom button.

'Yes?'

'Dell Weston leaving room seventy-four.

Notify my personal guard and call a fleet car.'

'Yes, sir.'

The guard was waiting when Dell left the elevator. He was a tall neatly-uniformed man, one of the house guards temporarily assigned to personal service. He saluted as he recognised Dell.

'Good morning, sir.' He hesitated. 'Sorry to hear of what happened to your wife, sir. A tragic loss.'

'Yes,' said Dell, emotionlessly. 'Is the car here?'

'One moment.' The guard walked to the exit, his young strong body seeming to strain at the black leather of his uniform. He nodded to the armed doorman, and hurried over to the waiting turbo-powered car. Opening the rear door he glanced within, then at the driver, then towards both ends of the thick concrete canopy shielding the exit of the building. He turned and gestured towards Dell.

'All clear, sir.'

'Good. Ride in front, will you.' Dell slid into the soft cushions of the rear compartment and slammed the door on the guard's protest. With a smooth whine from the turbine the car slid from beneath the canopy and into the sparse traffic of the city.

He rested against the soft cushions, not paying any attention to the route they took or the speed at which they travelled. His eyes burned and his head throbbed with a dull ache. He had a sour taste in his mouth and wished that it was possible to avoid the coming interview with his partner, but that was impossible. Bender meant to force him to a decision, and somehow he felt that he lacked the moral courage to hold out any longer.

The car hesitated at a high barrier, then slid into the building proper. The guard swung down from his seat opened the door, and, hand resting lightly on the butt of his holstered pistol, walked closely beside Dell as he passed the humming workshops and entered the administration offices.

'I shan't be needing you for a while. Wait in the refreshment room.'

'But, sir . . . '

'Please. This is my factory. I am

surrounded by friends. I'll call you when I need you.'

The young man hesitated, then shrugged, and saluting, turned on his heel and walked stiffly away. Dell watched him with a wry grin; if he should happen to die, he was certain of at least one mourner.

Bender was waiting in the inner office.

He looked drawn and a muscle high on one cheek jumped and writhed beneath his sallow skin. Like Dell, he was dressed in blouse, jacket and trousers with a sash about his waist, but there the similarity ended. His trousers were of a screaming orange, his sash a deep maroon and his blouse a sickly violet. His short jacket matched the cloak hung near the door, being a combination jazz and rainbow pattern. He also wore two long-barrelled pistols belted around his waist.

'I'd almost given you up,' he smiled. 'What happened, did Madge keep you this morning?'

'Madge is dead,' said Dell quietly.

'What!' Bender half rose from his chair, then sank back into his seat shaking his head. 'Man, but you took a chance!'

'I didn't kill her,' snapped Dell. 'An assassin shot at me last night, missed, and the bullet hit Madge.'

'An assassin? But how?'

'I opened the window,' confessed Dell. 'I didn't imagine that I'd be in any personal danger, but someone must have been waiting for me to make a slip.' He hung up his cloak, and joined his partner at the desk. 'I don't want to talk about it any more.'

'Did you get a signed deposition?'

'I said that I didn't want to talk about it.'

'Sorry.' Bender reached beneath his jacket and when his hand reappeared he held a small, intricately carved box. He pressed a spring and the lid flew open exposing a little mound of white powder. Delicately he lifted a pinch on the nail of his thumb and carefully sniffed it up each nostril. Dell frowned his displeasure.

'Do you have to take the stuff, Bender?'

'Why not? It gives me a lift, and what the hell! I can afford it.'

'Seeing as how we manufacture it, I

don't doubt it.' Dell tried not to sound sarcastic. His morals were his own and if he wished them respected, then he had to respect those of others. If a man wanted to sniff cocaine early in the morning, then that was nothing to do with him or any man.

Bender sighed contentedly as he replaced the box within his jacket. He seemed much calmer, the muscle had ceased twitching and his hard grey eyes glittered with sheer vitality. He laughed at Dell's expression.

'Don't be such an old man, Dell. Sure, I know all the arguments why I shouldn't sniff coke, but what does that get me? Sure I'll become an addict, I'm one now. Sure it'll give me the screaming meemies, but not as long as I can get the stuff and that will be always. If my health breaks too soon then I'll go for a cure, but in the meantime live and let live.'

'As you say, Bender.' Dell fumbled in his pockets and took out a crumpled package. Defiantly he lit the cigarette, trying not to see Bender's look of amusement.

'Tobacco isn't addictive,' he said, half guiltily.

'Certain it isn't?' Bender grinned. 'What do you do when you can't get any?'

'Do without,' snapped Dell. 'I can take it or leave it alone.'

'You're lucky,' admitted his partner. 'I can't and neither can a lot of other people.' He became serious. 'I want to talk to you, Dell, a real talk I mean, and I've someone here to help me do it.'

'What do you mean?'

'I've called in an arbitrator. Now don't get upset, but things have reached a stage where we just can't go on like this any longer. You know that we had another raid last night?'

'So you told me.'

'Yes. Yes so I did, I'd forgotten. Well, McKeefe reports that the guards are going to demand an extra bonus for running unnecessary risk. They know what is behind all these raids, and they don't feel as if their pay is enough to warrant them getting shot at for no good reason.'

'Then get other guards.'

'Are you serious, Dell? You know as well as I do that McKeefe's men are psycho-tested and respect the Ethical Contract. Do you want a crew of guards who will open the doors to the Anti's or just raid the store themselves?'

'Then pay the bonus.'

'With what?' Bender smiled and slowly shook his head.

'Get wise, Dell. The fiddling amounts of cocaine we sell to the hospitals wouldn't pay that extra for a month. As it is we are running on a shoestring, we've got to expand.'

'No.'

'But, Dell . . . '

'I said no, and I mean that.'

'All right, Dell, but I have something to say about that. I'm your partner remember.'

'Not a controlling one.'

'Maybe not, but my money is in this business and I've a right to protect my investment.'

'What do you intend to do?'

'Can you buy me out?'

'No.' Dell bit his lips as he tried to

control his mounting impatience. He couldn't blame Bender too much, the man was within his rights at protesting at what seemed to him to be a raw deal, but somehow Dell couldn't understand why he appeared to be so wantonly blind as to refuse to se the obvious,

'I'm going to be fair with you, Dell.' Bender leaned across the table, his eyes glittering and hard. 'I'm going to submit our case for arbitration. Will you abide by the decision?'

Dell hesitated, to refuse would be a confession of doubt in the wholesomeness of what he felt to be right. To agree would be to bind himself to the unbiased opinion of a third party, and he shrank from what that opinion might be.

'Well?' Bender was getting impatient.

'Who is it?'

'Does that matter?' Bender laughed contemptuously. 'I haven't fixed him, if that's what you mean. He's a government man, recommended by the business bureau, you can psycho-test him if you like. Well?'

'Bring him in,' surrendered Dell, and

felt a tremendous lifting of responsibility.

'Good man!' Bender smiled and reached for the squat box of the intercom. 'Send in the Arbitrator,' he snapped into the speaker, 'and see that this section of the building is sealed.'

'Yes, sir.' The operator sounded tired and lifeless. 'Sir!'

'What is it?'

'Would it be possible for me to have an advance of salary — in kind?'

'See the section supervisor, why bother me with such matters?'

'I did, sir. My request was refused.'

'Well?'

'But I must have some, sir. I'm desperate for it. Please, sir, I'll do anything, anything at all.'

Bender winked at the stony face of his partner, and deliberately opened the circuit. 'Let her sweat for a while,' he said callously, 'soon she'll really mean what she says, and then we'll have her working for a few sniffs a week.'

Dell didn't smile. Reaching across the desk he thumbed the switch of the intercom and snapped terse orders.

'Supervisor! Discharge the intercom operator. Discharge all addicts, immediate notice!' His face softened. 'Give them one grain each with their salary.'

Bender grinned at him, his grey eyes glittering and hard, but there was no mirth in his smile.

'You're a fool, Dell, a stupid, blind fool. Do you think that those people will thank you for what you've done?'

'Maybe not, but you offer them even less than that.'

'You know that they're addicts, working here they can get the stuff at cost, outside they'll have to beg, rob, murder for it. Haven't you enough enemies, Dell?'

'I can handle them.'

'Can you? Maybe next time the assassin won't miss.'

Dell stared at his partner, sudden suspicion springing to ugly life in the dim recess of his mind. Unconsciously he tensed, feet shifting to gain better traction on the smooth floor if the need for sudden movement arose. Bender watched him with his glittering cat's eyes, and reluctantly shook his head.

'I won't kill you, Dell. It would be easy, too easy, but we're partners and the Contract would force the others to kill me too. No, Dell, you're safe enough, killing you just wouldn't be worth it.'

'Don't let the Contract stop you.' Dell felt the swift surge of almost uncontrollable anger. 'I'll sign a deposition of mutual decision, then lend me one of your guns and we'll see who kills whom.'

'No, Dell. Not that way, it would be murder, you aren't used to arms.' Abruptly Bender laughed, a deep sound of pure amusement, and irrationally Dell felt his anger drain away.

Softly the door opened behind them.

3

He was dressed all in grey, a cold neutral colour, the shade of snow-laden clouds, the storm-tossed sea, the grey of limitless distance and of dead hope. His eyes were grey, his hair, even his skin seemed to have the same leaden hue as his simple clothing. He stood just within the open door, and for a startled moment Dell thought that he stared at a ghost, then the stranger moved and the spell was broken.

'Messrs. Dell and Bender? I am the Arbitrator; I believe that one of you gentlemen sent for me.'

'I did.' Bender rose and extended his hand. 'Glad to see you Mister . . . ?'

'Lassiter. Eric Lassiter.'

'Thank you. My name is Bender, and this is my partner, Dell Weston. Take a chair will you, and let's get down to business.'

'As you wish.' Lassiter sat down between the two men and spilled papers from a grey leather briefcase on to the polished surface of the desk. He looked at the partners, 'Have you a recording instrument here?'

'Yes.' Dell gestured towards a portable recorder. 'Do you want it switched on?'

'If you please.' The tall, grey man waited as Dell turned on the instrument. 'Go ahead.'

'My name is Eric Lassiter, and I am recognised Arbitrator for the settlement of business and personal disputes. I have been psycho-tested and am without fear or prejudice. This is case one-thousand-and-eight, discussed on the twenty-second of November, 2087. Parties in the dispute are Dell Weston and his business partner, Jeff Bender. Is that correct, gentlemen?'

'Correct.' Bender leaned a little towards the recorder.

'Correct.' Dell snapped the single word, then leaned back fumbling for his cigarettes.

'The dispute is a business one. The controlling partner, Dell Weston, insists that the product of his factory, refined cocaine, should be restricted in sale to hospitals and medical personnel. The minor partner, Jeff Bender, sees no reason why in the normal course of good business the cocaine should not be offered for free sale to all. As Arbitrator, I have been called to decide the issue. Do both of you gentlemen agree to abide by my opinion?'

'Yes.'

'I do.'

'You both realise that if either of you should not agree to my opinion, then the other may regard himself free of the Ethical Contract, and be free to take what steps he wishes without fear of retribution?'

'If Dell doesn't agree, then I will kill him.'

'If your opinion is in my favour, then I will regard our partnership ended, unless, of course, Bender agrees to allow me full control of the factory.'

'I see that you both understand the position. Now may I have your arguments for and against please.'

Dell hesitated, looking at Bender. Jeff shrugged.

'I'll speak first.' He leaned close to the recorder.

'To me the question is a simple one. We are businessmen, and naturally wish to make a profit by selling our product. There can be no moral or legal objection to offering anything for free sale, on the contrary, we are morally bound to do so. To refuse to place our drug on the open market is to encourage crime and to create unhappiness.' He leaned back with a gesture and reached for his little carved box. The Arbitrator glanced at Dell.

'To offer cocaine for free sale is to create a demand for a harmful drug. Drug addicts are dangerous both to themselves and to others, and supplying the drug would cause great distress. From experience gathered by watching the effects of the free sale of opium and marijuana I know that children, women and working people will become addicts to their own, and the community's loss. I feel a moral obligation to keep cocaine out of irresponsible hands.' He sighed and nodded at the tall figure of the grey man.

Lassiter sat silent for a moment, then

reaching out turned the control of the recorder. He smiled and relaxed from his semi-official attitude.

'I can see what is the trouble, and I don't think that we need to bother to record all our conversation. You, Dell, are a moralist. You, Bender, are a normal businessman. It is merely a matter of adjusting your points of view.'

'What is your opinion?' Bender clicked shut the lid of his box and glared impatiently at the tall grey man. Lassiter smiled.

'A moment please. I don't think that we need have any unpleasantness over this, so with your permission, I'd like to settle the whole thing amicably.'

'Is it necessary?' Bender shrugged and examined his nails with minute care. 'What are you going to do, read him a lecture on the facts of life?'

'Something like that.' Lassiter smiled again, and turned to face the older man. 'Dell, as you know, I've no real power, the government now is merely a go-between and a court of moral appeal, we have no power to enforce any decision we may make, but haven't you ever stopped to think why that should be?'

'Why should I? It's natural isn't it?'

'Now it is, but it wasn't always so. About thirty years ago, Dell, things were far different. The government then had absolute power over the individual. Freedom was just a word with no real meaning, or if it had a meaning, it was freedom to think as ordered — or else. That was about the time when several groups of nations were getting ready for the final war, they had atomic weapons you know, and there was little doubt that civilisation was on the way out.' The tall grey man stared before him for a moment, his cold eyes misty with thought.

'Something happened then, Dell. What it was exactly no one will ever really know, but suddenly, all at the same time all over the world, all atomic weapons disintegrated in a cloud of radioactive glory. The great stockpiles of bombs, dusts, raw ores, all went up in smoke, and the atom war had finished before it could even start.'

'That's history,' snapped Bender. 'Hurry it up will you?'

'That's history,' agreed Lassiter, 'but the history of yesterday can explain the problems of today. You see, Dell, whatever was happening didn't just stop at the destruction of the atomic weapons — men changed too. Soldiers looked around them and for the first time really asked themselves just what the hell they thought they were doing. They drifted away from the armies, they drifted back home — and they took their guns with them. It didn't stop there. Civilians, ordinary people, began to ask themselves some very important questions. They wanted to know just why they had to do as they were told. Why couldn't they have a drink at any time of the day or night, why did they have to read censored literature, see censored films, wear conservative clothing? Why couldn't they be really free? A group of smart politicians swept to power; on the election promise of a really free world without petty restrictions — and found that they had to keep those promises. Tell me, Dell, are you free?'

'Yes, at least, I suppose that I am.'

'You wouldn't like anyone telling you

that tobacco is bad for you, and that you mustn't smoke because someone you've never even heard of decides that you mustn't?'

'Of course I wouldn't, but this is a different thing.'

'Is it? Freedom cannot be measured, Dell. Either you are free or you are not free, you cannot be half free, or a quarter or an eighth. All or none, Dell, all or none.'

'And so . . . ?'

'People must have the option of buying what they want, when they want, and people must have the right to sell what they like, when they like, and at the price they choose. You cannot stop Bender from offering your product for free sale.'

'But the results!'

'Would they be so very different? Hospitals and medical men are human, they buy cocaine — and sell it for what they can get. If it wasn't for your agreement with other manufacturers giving you sole right of this market, you would have been bankrupt long ago.'

'So you agree with Bender then?'

'Yes, Dell, I must.'

For a moment Dell sat silently fighting the turmoil of frustrated emotion boiling within him. He tried not to see his partner's look of triumph, and resisted the desire to refuse to agree. He knew that he would live just long enough for the Arbitrator to record his dissension, then Bender would smash his body with high velocity slugs. He swallowed.

'Very well. Morally I still think that you are wrong, but I'm forced to agree.'

Lassiter nodded with quiet satisfaction, and switched on the recorder.

'After conversation with both parties, my decision is that the cocaine products of this factory should be offered for free and unlimited sale. In this decision I side with the minor partner, Bender. Both partners agree to my opinion.'

'Confirmed.' Dell forced himself to sound pleasant.

'Confirmed!' Bender jumped from his seat, his hard young face wreathed with smiles. 'Good work, Lassiter. I knew that you'd see things my way. If there's anything I can do for you, anything you want? No? Then excuse me please, I'm going to see about increased output and arrange for city-wide distribution.' The door slammed behind him, cutting off the sound of his rapid footsteps, and the tall grey man smiled understandingly at Dell.

'Disappointed?'

'Yes.'

'That's a pity. The trouble with you, Dell, is that you're an idealist, and there just isn't a place in this world for idealists — not now.'

'I know what is right.'

'I'm sure you do, that's just the trouble with idealists, they are so certain they know what is best for others. So certain, that they will do anything to enforce their ideals — for the common good of course, but the methods they condone in order to reach their aims make normal men tremble. Do you remember the Spanish Inquisition, Dell? The Inquisition was staffed with idealists, men convinced that they were right — and you know what taste it left in history. The Nazis, the Communists, the Capitalists, the Socialists, the Church, all founded and expanded by men absolutely sincere and certain that what they brought to the world was unalloyed good.'

'Aren't you exaggerating a little?'

'Am I? Think a while, Dell. Think of a man driven by a single purpose, and remember that man is convinced that what he hopes to do will be to bring happiness to the majority. Tobacco is harmful to the health, therefore ban smoking, make tobacco illegal — and a healthy race will live to thank its saviour. Men are unable to think for themselves, therefore it would be kinder to do all their thinking for them — and a slave state worships its dictator. There are too many examples of idealists bringing the world to the edge of ruin. More misery, unhappiness, wanton waste and heartless cruelty has been committed in the name of idealism than for any other cause.'

'I still think that you're exaggerating. What has this to do with my desire to retain control of a habit-forming drug?'

'You miss the point. Dell. I'm not arguing with your motives, I'm against your self-opinionated conviction that you are the one able to decide what is good for your neighbour.'

'But if there is no one to worry about others, what then?'

'Liberty, Dell. Pure liberty for the very first time in recorded history. Each man must make his own decision, and none must try to persuade by threat or by punishment. If a man wishes to become a drug addict, then let him, he does so because he wants to, he hasn't been forced either way. Each must do as they wish, when they wish, and how they wish, that is the only real freedom.'

'Jungle law.' Dell said acidly.

'No. Tell me, Dell, you are at perfect liberty to go out into the street and kill the first passerby. Why don't you do it?'

'Why should I? Whoever it might be hasn't injured me, why should I kill for the sheer sake of killing?'

'Exactly. You don't kill because you have no reason to kill. There is no good reason for you to lie, to steal, to rob and destroy. Reason, Dell. Reason! That is why true freedom can never be jungle law.'

'There is another reason why I don't rob or kill,' Dell said drily. 'Retribution. If I were to shoot the first passerby, I am just as likely to be shot down in turn. If I attempt to rob someone, then that someone will almost certainly kill me. I don't do these things, Lassiter, because I'm fond of my own skin.'

'And you don't take drugs for the same reason. That is one thing about pure freedom, Dell. It sifts the sane from the insane, the reasoning intellects from the purely emotional. It also makes a civilisation truly adult.'

Dell frowned, staring at the calm features of the tall man, trying to sense a hidden meaning in the otherwise casual words. There was something strange about this man, something inexplicable and yet not at all disturbing. He looked again at the smooth grey hair, the calm grey eyes, the easy carriage and clear skin of the man, skin which belonged to a much younger person, and yet Lassiter could not be a young man. Arbitrators never were.

He shrugged. 'I wouldn't know about

that, I can't remember back before the change.'

'Of course not, I doubt if you were born then, but believe me, Dell, things aren't so very different. There were killers then, and thieves, and drug addicts. Men haven't changed all that much, but now they defend themselves instead of paying armies and huge police forces to do it for them. Arming the populace hasn't turned men into criminals, but disarming the people merely served to arm the gangsters and thugs. When each man is armed and ready to deal death, then anyone breaking the moral code is liable to pay the full penalty, and the moral code is the only one worth living under.'

'I still think that things were better in the old days. A man could leave his home then, and not fear that he would return to an empty shell. Assassins didn't kill innocent women, and what business employed armed guards? No, Lassiter, the old days had much to commend them.'

'The old days always have, but that is a natural trick of the memory. A man now has a chance to get what he can — if he can, and it is up to the property owners to guard themselves and their property. Civilisation is a vital thing, Dell, a growing thing. It must progress, or sink into decadence, it cannot remain static, and any civilisation must be measured by its smallest unit — the individual. If any member of any civilisation cannot claim freedom, then that civilisation is a slave state. If any member of any race cannot claim personal pride, freedom of choice, freedom to avenge personal wrongs, and yes, the right to go to hell in his own particular way, then that race has failed to mature. The strong cannot carry the weak, Dell, that path leads to the grave of hope and high endeavour.'

'I still say jungle law.'

'You are free to think what you like,' admitted the Arbitrator. He took the spool from the recorder and placed it within his grey leather case. 'I'll transcribe this and return the wiped spool.' He rose from the chair. 'I'm glad that you agreed to my opinion, Dell, your partner was in no mood for defiance.'

'He would have killed me.' Dell rose from his own seat. 'He still may.'

'Doesn't the Ethical Contract prevent that?'

'Theoretically, yes, but the Ethical Contract is, after all, only ethical. An employee mustn't steal from his employer, a business partner mustn't rob his associates, a guard must remain loyal to the person he is guarding or to the group who pays him. The penalty is to be hunted down by all other groups, a mutual agreement between business, guards and individuals. For theft of a petty nature, physical punishment, for serious theft or murder, death. Simple, but like most things, not always easy to enforce.'

'And yet it works.'

'Yes.'

Lassiter glanced at a thin wristwatch and held out his hand. 'Goodbye, Dell. If you're ever in trouble look me up, you know where to find me, Central Records, just off the business section.'

'Thanks.' Dell led the way towards the door. 'I'll remember that, but if ever I'm in that sort of trouble I'm afraid that you couldn't be of much use.' He sighed and angrily shook himself.

'Goodbye.'

The door swung softly shut behind the tall grey man, and tiredly Dell fumbled for his cigarettes. The inter-com hummed and impatiently he closed the circuit.

'Yes?'

'McKeefe here, sir. Do you want to examine the bodies before we get rid of them?'

'The bodies?'

'Yes, sir. The raiders of last night. Do you want to see them?'

'No. Wait!' Dell frowned in thought. 'Maybe I'd better. I'll meet you at the compound in five minutes. Has Bender seen them?'

'Yes, sir.'

'Five minutes then.'

The instrument clicked into silence.

4

They lay silent on the soiled concrete of the compound, three of them, all men. They rested face upwards, their open eyes gazing at the sullen bank of leaden clouds, their thin and wasted bodies ugly in rags and stained with dirt.

The rain glistened in little droplets on their waxen flesh, trickling from unkempt hair and tracing little paths in the dirt of their faces and hands. They didn't mind, not now, they were all very dead.

Dell stood in the rain and looked down at them, drawing his cloak closer around him, and trying not to see the ugly wounds caused by the high velocity bullets of the guards.

McKeefe, a thick-set middle-aged man, grunted as he gestured towards the bodies.

'Simple enough, sir. They were desperate, probably starving and mad enough to take any chance.'

'You think so?'

'Certain of it. Look.' He pointed at one of the bodies.

Across the dirt-stained forehead a red streak stood out like a thing alive. 'That one's branded, a petty offender against the Contract, but he'd never be able to get another job, and look, see how that other one has been branded with blue. A debtor.' The big man shrugged. 'Scum, the lot of them, no loss to anyone.'

'You don't think that the raid was planned by the Anti's then?'

'No. Not they, they would be glad to see the factory destroyed, but they wouldn't work that way, and neither would a business enemy. These raiders tried a lone chance, and they didn't have a chance, not with my guards on duty anyway.'

Dell caught the hidden inflexion in the otherwise casual tones of the Head Guard.

'You'll be glad to hear that we've decided to go into full production, McKeefe. Cocaine will be offered for sale to anyone who has the money to buy, men, women; yes, even children.'

'Good!' McKeefe smiled, his broad red face creasing with sheer pleasure. 'I'd have hated to revoke our contract Mr. Weston, but if you hadn't decided as you have, then I'd have taken my guards from the factory. I don't mind taking a normal risk, but things were getting out of hand. Did you know that we've shot over thirty raiders in the past eight weeks?'

'As many as that?'

'Yes, sir. Mister Bender said not to trouble you about it.'

'I see.' Dell stared down at the crumpled figures lying on the soiled concrete. 'Very well, McKeefe, you know what to do.'

'Yes, sir.' The big guard touched the brim of his padded uniform helmet and stared curiously at his employer's retreating figure. He shrugged, then with sudden irritation kicked at the bodies lying before him.

A man was waiting in the office when Dell returned. A small agile looking man, soberly dressed and with a peculiar bird-like quality to his sharp little features. He jumped up from his seat as the door opened, and extended a card, smiling at the same time.

'Mister Weston, sir? I am a representative of a new Service, Guaranteed Employers, Inc. Guarem offers an entirely new and comprehensive service to all employers of labour anywhere.'

'Not interested,' snapped Dell.

'Let me tell you of our service, sir. We undertake to recompense all loss caused by theft, fire, laxity of guards, and carelessness of personnel. For one all-inclusive fee, Mister Weston, you can relax and forget all your petty worries over personnel and guard details.'

'Excuse me, please, but I'm really not interested.'

'You can't afford not to be interested, sir. Let me explain.' The little man pulled his chair nearer to the wide desk. 'Once you have signed our agreement, we take full charge of all staff and guard problems. If you need more staff you tell us, if you wish to reduce your commitments, we take care of it. I find it impossible, Mister Weston, to understand

how any businessman cannot be interested in our offer.'

'I am beginning to understand. If I
agree, then you take charge of my staff?'

'Yes, sir, and guards also.'

'You psycho-test them, of course?'

'Naturally.'

'Of course, and I suppose that you have
full control over them?'

The little man frowned. 'I don't quite
understand, sir. How do you mean?'

'I mean that you decide who is to be
employed, at what rate of pay, hours of
labour and conditions of employment?'

'Yes, but remember, sir, we are insuring
you against all forms of loss caused by
inefficient staff.'

'A nice racket.' Dell glanced at his
wristwatch. 'Thank you, but I cannot
detain you any longer. You know the way
out.'

The little man flushed, and bit his lip. 'I
take offence at your tone, sir. Guarem is
not a racket, but a perfectly legitimate
business enterprise. All we are offering is
to relieve employers of staff problems.'

'By making virtual slaves of the staff?'

'This is a free world, sir. We force none to work for us.'

'No, but you can black-list a man, prevent him offering his labour to anyone else on your list. If I agreed to sign then what happens to my staff?'

'We take over. They would be psycho-tested for loyalty, re-graded for salary, medically examined for health.'

'What of those who fail your tests?'

'Discharged, sir, naturally. We cannot afford to take any risks.'

'No. No. I suppose not. You may go now.'

'But . . . '

'Are you protected by the Ethical Contract?' Dell smiled as he stared at the little man. 'I didn't ask you to come here, you are not my partner, I owe you nothing. Now get out!'

'Really, Mister Weston!'

'Get out or I'll have you thrown out!'

Irritably Dell thumbed a button on the desk before him. Within seconds the door burst open and the tall figure of his personal guard stood just within the room, his glittering pistol menacing the shrinking figure of the little man.

'Show him out,' snapped Dell.

'Yes, sir.' The pistol jerked as the tall young guard gestured towards the representative: 'Come on now.'

'Very well.' For a moment anger glittered in the little eyes and the sharp features. The Guarem representative picked up his briefcase, and nodded curtly towards Dell.

'You may regret this, Mister Weston, you may regret this quite a lot.'

Dell shrugged, and forgot him the moment the door closed.

The intercom hummed and Bender's sharp voice echoed from the speaker.

'Dell. I'm coming up to have a conference. Are you alone?'

'Yes.'

'Good, be there in three minutes.'

It was nearer ten before Bender thrust open the door and crossed the room with jerky steps. His sallow face was flushed and his cold eyes held a hard glitter. He sat down, then jumped up almost immediately, crossing to the window then back to the desk. Dell stared at him with mounting irritation.

'Sit down man, sit down before you make me as jumpy as yourself. What's on your mind?'

'Production, Dell, that's what.' Bender seated himself and fumbled for his little carved box. His hand trembled and some of the fine white powder spilled onto the polished surface of the wide desk. Impatiently he scooped up more and sniffed at his loaded thumbnail.

'Better now?' Dell didn't even try to hide his disgust, and his partner flushed angrily.

'Damn you, Dell, for the toffee-nose you are, but I didn't come here to exchange insults.'

'Then what did you come for?'

'To discuss future plans. Listen. Now that you've finally seen sense and agreed to sell on a free market, we've got to make plans. My idea is this. We'll step up production to the limit, flood the city with cocaine at a price as cheap as we can afford, below cost if we have to, anything to create a demand. Then when we've created that demand, we lift the price as far as we dare, and from then on live in gravy.'

He frowned thoughtfully, scribbling figures on a scratchpad.

'We must be careful about setting the final price. Low enough so that it wouldn't pay others to attempt to smuggle into our market, and low enough so that we don't put it beyond reach of the mass consumer, at the same time we want it high enough to yield the maximum amount of profit. The way I see it, the price would be set at a level so that anyone can buy a little, but few people can afford to buy in bulk. We'd better get some market research done, I'll give the contract to a recommended firm, they've had experience with the marijuana trade.'

Dell stared at his young partner and tried not to smile. Bender caught his expression and frowned suspiciously.

'What's amusing you, Dell? Something up your sleeve?'

'No. I think that your plan is a good one, a simple business proposition, and to hell with the addicts such a plan must produce. I don't like it, Bender, but I won't have to worry about it.'

'No?'

'No. Your plan depends on flooding the market, and that means money, lots of money. Where are you going to get it from?'

'Us, of course, we'll pour in every cent we have. Man, with a thing like this we can't lose!'

'I know that, but I haven't any money. My inclusive rent takes almost all I draw from the business. Madge took the rest, at least, she did when she was alive. I can't help you, Bender.'

'Damn!' The young man frowned down at the polished surface of the table. 'I haven't any spare cash.' He looked at Dell. 'How much would we need?'

'It depends. We could sell off all existing stocks, buy raw materials with the proceeds, and increase our turnover. To flood the market means accumulating stocks, buying raw materials, paying salaries, the guards, a dozen things, and that would take far more than we could ever hope to raise.'

'I see.' Bender scribbled at the white

surface of the scratchpad. 'It looks as if we must raise a loan.'

'At one-hundred per cent interest? You know that's what banks charge when they know a firm is desperate.'

'Wait a moment!' Bender stared at Dell his sallow cheeks red with excitement. 'Didn't Madge leave you anything? Didn't you have a joint insurance policy?'

'What if we did?' Dell stared at his partner feeling his temper surge at the callous disregard of his feelings. Madge was dead, had died scant hours before, and within a day she was being forgotten. Forgotten that is but for what wealth she may have left.

'Then we'll use that money. We may not be able to flood the market, but we can at least avoid mortgaging the firm to a bank.'

'No!'

'No?' Bender looked his surprise. 'Why not? We're partners aren't we? I have a right to that money, and you know it. Don't start getting funny ideas, Dell, this thing means too much to me for anything to stand in the way.'

'Then why not kill me too?' Dell stared

at the young man not troubling to disguise his contempt. 'We also have a joint policy, and as my next-of-kin you'd get all I own.'

'Don't mention that!' Bender half rose from his seat one hand dropping to the butt of a pistol. 'Don't ever mention that again, don't even think it. I'm not related to you, neither of our parents were the same. My father shot yours in an honest disagreement, then married your mother out of pity. You and I were grown then, you a few years older than I, and my father always favoured you.'

'That is a lie! Your father liked me, but don't think that I ever forgave him for what he did to my father. I was ten then, and I can remember how my mother felt when they told her what had happened. We almost starved, we almost froze and every time I heard a gun fire. I couldn't stop trembling for hours. What else could my mother do but marry again?'

'Well they're both dead now, and that is old history, but you know how I feel about it, Dell. Just don't remind me again.'

'Dead, yes, both dead, and how? Shot by a half-crazy drug addict craving for dope! Doesn't that warn you against flooding the city with cocaine?'

'That has nothing to do with it.' Bender jerked from his chair and began to stride the room. The muscle twitched again high on his cheek and he constantly bit his lip in a frenzy of emotion. Dell watched him, his eyes softening as he stared at the over-tense young man.

'Sit down, Jeff. Take another sniff if you feel like it, don't let's quarrel now.'

'That's good of you! Damn you, Dell, do you have to be so smug? I know what cocaine is doing to me, but I can't do without it! Can't you understand, damn you? I can't do without it!'

'Then take some, but stop jittering around!'

Bender stopped, trembling with sheer rage, his hands hovering like claws above the twin butts of his pistols. His eyes glittered and his lips writhed from his teeth. When he spoke his voice sounded like glass paper rubbing on sand.

'I love all you self-satisfied smug little people. You know just what is wrong with the world, don't you? You know best, you always know best, but, damn you, how can you know? How can you know how I feel, how all the rest of the world feels? You've never lived, you sit smug and sneering wrapped in your own conceit and feel a little sorry for all us poor fools who do what we shouldn't. Why aren't you armed, Dell? Why don't you carry a gun? Would it be because you're afraid of using one? An unarmed man is a coward, Dell, a dirty stinking coward, and that's just what you are!'

'Sit down!'

'Go to hell!'

Abruptly Dell stood up from his chair, sending it skidding several feet across the smooth floor from the force of his rising. He stepped forward, his body crouched, his eyes narrowed, feeling the increased pounding of his heart as rage suddenly mastered him.

Bender stared at him, his hard young face sneering, one hand jerking at a holstered weapon.

'Get back, Dell! Dell! Don't make me kill you!'

The gun thudded against the floor as Dell smashed it from his partner's hand. Deliberately he drew back his fist and felt a rush of satisfaction as he drove it full into Bender's face. The young man screamed with anger and clawed desperately at his second pistol.

He never drew it. Dell struck again, sinking his fist deep into the soft flesh of the stomach, and snatching the gun from a nerveless hand threw it behind him. He drew a long shuddering breath.

'Now, Jeff,' he whispered. 'Let's see just how much of a coward I am.' Deliberately he moved forward.

Bender kicked, his knee-boot gleaming in the light as it swept towards Dell's groin, the metal-tipped sole flashing in a sharp arc. Dell twisted, taking the force of the blow on one thigh, his leg numbing beneath the force of the impact. He grabbed for the boot, missed, and stepped forward, his fists swinging.

Blows dashed against his face and head, but they were weak, without great strength, the futile blows of a man who had weakened his body with enervating drugs. He smashed his fist against the young man's pale features, feeling his knuckles split against teeth, and rejoicing in the sight of fresh-spilled blood. Again he drove short, savage blows into Bender's face, feeling the nose pulp into ruin, the lips split again, and feeling a dull ache in his knuckles as the force of his blows smashed teeth.

Bender fought with the spitting fury of a cornered rat, Dell with the bitter frustration of moral defeat. Dell fought to injure, Bender fought to kill. He stabbed with stiffened fingers and jerked viciously with his knee. Dell twisted his head, feeling nails tear at his cheek as they sought his eyes, then doubled, retching, as agony surged from his groin. He wavered for a moment, sick with pain, weakly trying to prevent Bender from gouging at his eyes, and feeling the dull thud of repeated blows and kicks.

Weakly he straightened, forcing the younger man back with a rain of blows to the face, then as his pain died to be replaced with anger, he stepped forward.

Beneath his fury Bender had no

chance. He doubled beneath a blow to his throat, straightened beneath an uppercut, and stood glassy-eyed and swaying as Dell slowly drew back his fist. The blow sounded strangely loud, and with a faint moan, Bender slumped to the floor, his violet blouse now mottled and stained with blood.

The door burst open, the alarmed faces of guards showing beyond the portal. Dell stared at them, then gestured towards the unconscious figure before him.

'Look after him will you, I'm going out.'

'Yes, sir.' A guard dropped on one knee beside the slumped figure. 'Where are you going, sir?'

'Where?' Dell smiled absently rubbing one hand over his split knuckles. 'To buy a gun.'

He walked from the office, not noticing his personal guard, and feeling strangely relieved.

5

The gunsmith looked a little like a vulture, with red-rimmed eyes and a back that had long curved into a permanent stoop. He was dressed in rust-coloured blouse and trousers with a wide black sash around his scrawny middle. He smiled and his teeth were black and stained with tobacco.

'Good afternoon, may I serve you?'

Dell shook the rain from his cloak, and looked around the small shop. Weapons hung on racks against the walls, more gleamed from glass cases, and boxed ammunition rested on shelves behind the counter. A guard, his face mottled and lined, his unifonn frayed and dingy, sat stolidly on a chair in one corner, chewing gum and nursing the squat barrel of an automatic sub-gun resting on his knee.

A shadow dimmed the light from the street, and Dell turned to face the hovering figure of his personal guard.

'I won't be needing you again. You may return to the business section.'

'Yes, sir. I'll wait outside if you wish.'

'Didn't you hear me? I said that you may return home now.'

'No, sir.' The young guard shifted uncomfortably and looked anywhere but at his employer. 'This is a dangerous section for a businessman, sir. I must stay with you.'

Dell sighed and shook his head.

'I shall be quite all right I tell you. I am going to buy a gun, then after a little walk through the city, I will return home. I assure you that you won't be needed.'

'I'm sorry, sir, but I must stay with you.'

'Look.' Dell was getting a little annoyed. 'I told you that I'm buying a gun.'

'Yes, sir, but begging your pardon, sir, having a gun and knowing how to use it are two different things.'

'As you wish.' Dell shrugged and turned to the little gunsmith. 'I want a gun, can you help me?'

'I believe so, sir.' The man's little

red-rimmed eyes glanced at the well-dressed figure of the businessman. Dell flushed as he felt the cold scrutiny, and automatically rubbed his forehead.

'What's the matter? Don't you want to serve me?'

'Of course, sir. It's only that sometimes a little care is necessary. I wouldn't sell a weapon to a branded man for example, nor would I sell to an Anti. A man has to be careful these days, as a businessman you must realise that.'

'You surprise me,' Dell said drily. 'I had the impression that the sole purpose of a shopkeeper was to sell his wares.'

'No, there I disagree. A shopkeeper distributes his wares, and I have the right to refuse to sell should I so decide.'

'I know that, now shall we get down to business?'

'Certainly. Now what sort of weapon would you like sir?'

'Just a gun. Something that you point at someone, pull the trigger, and kill him.'

The gunsmith smiled a little, and stared at the tall figure of Dell's personal guard as if they shared a private joke. The burly guard seated in the corner grunted, and noisily spat.

'What's wrong now?' snapped Dell irritably. He drew his cloak around him. 'Perhaps I'd better take my trade elsewhere.'

'No, sir. Forgive me please, but it is clear that you know little about guns.'

'Well?'

'Now which sort of weapon would best suit you, sir? A high-velocity twenty-five shot semi-automatic? A large calibre low-velocity revolver? A single shot derringer? A five millimetre? A seven? A nine? A point forty-five? Or would you like a semi-portable light automatic?'

Dell stared at the red-eyed smiling features and looked helplessly about him. Pistols lined the walls, rifles, squat-barrelled hand machine-guns, the variety seemed endless.

'What would you advise?'

'If I could assist, sir?' The tall figure of the personal guard stepped forward and leaned over the counter. 'A big pistol wouldn't be of much use to you, sir, you aren't used to them, and I doubt if you will ever need extreme range. You hardly want a machine pistol, and a small calibre weapon would be easier to fire. Unless you intend wearing holsters you don't want a big pistol at all, but at the same time a single shot isn't much use if you get into serious trouble.'

'I think that I have just the thing.' The gunsmith reached beneath his counter and gently placed a squat-barrelled weapon on the glass top. 'These are fairly new, designed to suit just such a person as yourself.' He broke open the gun and revealed three chambers. 'It fires a shot-gun shell, small charge and has specially strengthened chambers. The load is a dozen three-millimetre shot, the range about fifty feet and the firing pattern is about a yard.'

Dell picked the gun up in his hand and felt the balance and weight.

'You notice the shape of the weapon, flat, and not too heavy, it could easily be carried beneath a sash. There is a single trigger, and the chambers alternate with each pull.' He demonstrated, clicking the oiled trigger as he displayed the weapon.

'Even a bad shot can hit a target with one of these, at close range the blast would almost tear the head off a man.'

'I'll take it,' decided Dell. 'Load it for me, will you.'

'One moment, sir.' The tall young guard picked up the weapon and held out his hand to the gunsmith. 'I'll load and test this weapon first if you don't mind.'

'Certainly. There is a firing range at the back.'

The guard nodded, and stepped through the indicated door. Dell heard three shots, they seemed muffled and not half as loud as he had expected. Three more shots echoed flatly from the range, then the guard returned, and nodded.

'A good weapon.'

'How much?' Dell pursed his lips at the price mentioned, but paid for the gun and a box of ammunition, slipping the loaded weapon beneath his sash. He drew his cloak around him, and stepped out into the rain.

'I want you to go back now,' he said to the guard 'I know all about your duties, but I want to be alone. I'll thumbprint a deposition to that effect.'

'But, sir . . . '

'I mean it,' snapped Dell.

'Very well, sir, as you wish.' The guard slipped a folder from beneath his cloak, and offered a form for Dell to sign and print. He glanced at his watch and noted the time and place.

'Shall I call a car for you, sir?'

'No, but call one for yourself, I'll pay.' Dell tried not to grin at the worried expression on the guard's face as he climbed reluctantly into the car and was whirled away. He smiled, and drew a deep breath. It was good not to have the ever-present shadow of the guard at his shoulder. It was too easy to rely on others, to feel an artificial fear and to imagine danger at every turn. He touched the smooth metal of the pistol beneath his sash, and wondered how it was that the mere possession of a weapon could give a man courage. He didn't know it, but he had merely traded one staff for another.

For a while he wandered about the streets, penetrating deeper and deeper into the squalid section of the city. The workers lived here, the labourers, the beggars and broken men. Here poverty walked and possession of goods was to invite sudden attack. He was too engrossed in his own thoughts to notice the glances thrown at him by unkempt men with hungry, desperate eyes.

A crowd had gathered on one corner, a mingling of men and women listening to an orator, perched on a side platform. Words came thinly to him, hot words carried on the chill wind and drawing him to the edge of the crowd. The speaker, he noticed with surprise, was a woman, a young woman with long black hair and a complexion unmarred by any trace of cosmetics. Three men stood at the base of the rough platform, they faced the crowd and handed leaflets to all who would take them, but not many did.

'I appeal to you,' shouted the woman, 'to stop this horrible trade. Is it good enough for you to see your wives and children sacrificed to the lust for money shown by these manufacturers and traders? Have you no fear when you see young men and women, yes even small children, half-crazed with drugs and desperate for more? What of their health you mothers? What of your pride you fathers? Can you be proud of a daughter raped by a drugged madman? Can you be proud of a son shot down like a dog for trying to satisfy an appetite created, deliberately created, by the makers of drugs? Can you blame them when you yourselves do nothing to stop this horrible traffic?'

A man next to Dell spat, and pulled half a cigarette from his pocket. He lit it, and the familiar odour of marijuana drifted on the rain-laden air.

'Fools!' he spat. 'Why can't they mind their own business?'

'Who are they?' Dell craned forward trying to see more clearly. The man grunted at the impact of an elbow in his ribs, and thrust Dell away from him.

'Take it easy fellow.'

'What?' Dell stared at him, and let his hand drop to the weapon in his sash. 'What did you say?'

The man noticed the slight gesture and became suddenly very polite. He jerked a dirty thumb at the speaker.

'Why doesn't someone stop these Antis? Always against something, trying to tell us just how we should live. If I had a gun I'd shoot her myself.'

'Would you?' Dell stared at the man. 'Why?'

'Why? You should hear my wife and then you'd know why. Never a minute's peace, always nagging about what I spend on cigarettes, won't even let me drink or go to the strip-films now, and all because of people like that.' He stared thoughtfully at Dell. 'You have a gun, haven't you, don't deny it, I can tell when a man's armed. Why don't you blast her down?'

'She doesn't bother me.'

'She will do, friend. You're a businessman, aren't you? Well she's against all businessmen. Personally I don't care one way or the other, one day I'll go up into the business section and grab myself a handful of what I want. I only want a gun to do it with, just let me get my hands on a gun, and then you'll see who's the boss around here.'

He walked away muttering to himself,

his eyes glazed with the drug-induced euphoria. Dell shrugged and turned away. A man stepped into his path.

He was ragged and thin and looked terribly ill. His hair hung lankly about his narrow forehead and he wore an idiotic drooling grin. Saliva trickled down from one corner of his mouth, and his eyes were like glowing coals in the fish-belly whiteness of his face. A streak of brilliant crimson blazed his forehead, and his claw-like hands quivered with incessant motion.

He leered, and waved his jerking hands at Dell.

'I knows yer, I knows yer I tell yer. I knows yer.'

Dell stopped, looking around him, and trying to ignore the drooling thing before him. The man stepped closer, and hastily Dell stepped backwards, his stomach twisting in revulsion.

'Gimme some money. I wants some money. I knows yer, I tells yer, I knows yer.'

A man thrust his way past Dell's shoulder. Ragged, dirty, but with a physically powerful body and an unmarked face.

'Don't worry, sir. I'll guard you.' He thrust at the horrible thing standing before them. 'Get out of it. Be on your way now. Go on, move!'

Dell smiled tightly, watching the scene with cynical eyes.

He knew what was happening, had heard about it from others, but had never really experienced it himself before. It was a plant. The drooling, simple-minded man, an idiot, drug-crazed, but relatively harmless, and the strong protector. One would intimidate a likely prospect, the other would step forward offering his services as a guard, services that naturally had to be paid for, and well paid for.

He smiled, slipping the pistol from his sash and holding it ready beneath the shield of his cloak.

'You can cut it out now,' he snapped.

'What?' The big man turned and stared his surprise.

'You don't have to worry, sir. I'm your guard now, I'll see that you don't get hurt.'

'Thank you, but I can look after myself.' Dell let the cloak slip open and gestured slightly with the pistol. 'Want to argue about it?'

The man stared at him, his muscles writhing beneath his ragged clothing, then glanced down at the menacing eye of the pistol, and stepped back.

'No, I don't want to argue, but he might.' He jerked his head at the drooling idiot.

'What's the matter with him?'

'Hunger mostly, drug-hunger.' The big man laughed curtly. 'You wouldn't know about that, not where you come from. You've never known what it is to want something, really want it I mean. Luke's harmless enough, so you can put away your gun now, the trouble is that he has an addiction for a very expensive thing. Cocaine, you know of it? He was under medical treatment once, and they kept filling him with dope, his money ran out, and they kicked him into the street, but he had grown used to the drug. Now . . . ' He shrugged, and pulled gently at the idiot's arm.

'Come on, Luke, there's nothing here.'

'Wait!' Dell fumbled in his pocket, and

threw several coins at the big man. 'Buy him some food.'

Irritably he strode away.

First Madge, then Bender, the Arbitrator, and even the Anti speaker. What was wrong with the world that everyone seemed to be either interested in, or addicted to, dope in one form or another. Deep within himself he knew that it really wasn't so, he made the stuff, it was logical to suppose that he would move in circles with similar interests, but he could only see a fragment of the picture.

The majority didn't take drugs, didn't kill on sight, plan to rob and destroy. The majority were decent individuals living a decent normal life, it was he who was not normal. He shrugged and felt in his pockets for cigarettes; the packet was empty and he stopped at a booth.

'Cigarettes, please.'

'What sort? Tobacco, marijuana or opium?'

'Tobacco, Peerless, please.' He tore open the package and spun his lighter into flame. A man bumped into him and he moved away, drawing on the calming smoke, his mind still only half aware of what he was doing and where he was.

It must have always been like this, he thought. A majority of decent, clean-living people, and a smaller criminal element. There had always been drug addicts, there had always been those who tried to get what they wanted at the point of a gun, and there had always been idealists who had a certain remedy for the world — their remedy.

He grunted with surprise as someone bumped into him again, and stood motionless, glancing around and trying to recognise where he was.

He failed.

The area was new to him, a narrow alley twisting between high windowless buildings, dim and filled with shadows in the dying light. Rain trickled down the walls, splashing from open gutters and gathering in pools on the concrete path. He frowned, hesitated, then swinging on his heel began to retrace his path. He felt uncomfortable, the alley was too shadowy, too dim, too deserted for any man wearing good clothes to feel wholly safe, and he lengthened his stride, the sound of his heels making sharp ringing noises as they slapped the wet concrete.

Two men entered the alley, two slight-bodied, tense-faced men. They separated as they drew nearer, one passing to either side, and Dell felt a warning prickle irritate a spot between his shoulders. They weren't gutter scum, but neither were they businessmen. They moved with a simple efficiency, a smooth coordination of effort as if they had done this thing a thousand times before and knew exactly how it should be done.

Watching them, Dell tried to rationalise his fear. These men weren't thugs, they were probably upper-class workers in a hurry, but somehow he couldn't quite ignore the primeval warning of his tensed nerves, and he hesitated.

His hesitation almost proved fatal!

A loaded club swung at his head, hissing slightly as it clove through the wet air impelled with the full force of trained muscles. He ducked and twisted aside, desperately trying to save his skull from the shattering blow, almost slipping on the wet concrete. Pain lanced in a red wave of anguish from his shoulder as the club missed his head, numbing his entire left arm and seeming to have splintered the very bone.

Desperately he jerked to one side, tugging at the pistol and struggling with the hampering cloak. The club swung again, and the second man stepped forward, his tight hard features a mask of distaste at a job being badly done.

Dell swung aside the cloak, raised he pistol and pulled the trigger.

The gun thundered, the recoil jerking at his wrist and the sound startling him with its unexpected noise. The man stopped, his face in a twisted expression of pain and surprise. The pistol roared again, the blast directed at point-blank range towards the twisted features.

For a moment Dell stared at a red-stained skull, a pulped mass of flesh and bone, then something smashed against his head and blackness spun towards him.

6

Sounds whispered at him, a strange medley of blurred noise and metallic gratings. He stirred, whimpering a little from the pain in his head, and blinked as strong light seared his over-sensitive eyes with a brassy glare. Again the strange medley of sound, not whispering this time but with vibrant thunder, beating and pulsing in quivering grates of metal and soggy thuds mingled with the thin shouts of men.

He groaned and sat upright, feeling the rough surface of concrete rasp his naked flesh and the damp moisture of freezing rain chill his shivering body. He closed his eyes, resting his throbbing head between his hands and waited for the churning nausea gripping his stomach to fade and die.

'You there. Get up!'

'What?' Dell opened his eyes, narrowing them against the too-bright light and stared at the uniformed figure of a guard.

'You heard me.' The man leaned forward a little, bending from the hips, the long club in his hand ready for action.

'I've been watching you, now that you're awake be on your way.'

'Wait,' gasped Dell sickly. 'I've been attacked, robbed, beaten up. I'm sick.'

'That's your worry,' snapped the man impatiently. He peered closer and whistled as he saw the ugly swelling streaked with blood on the side of Dell's head.

'Say, you *have* been beaten up!' He shrugged. 'You probably asked for it, now get out of here before I take you in.'

'Wait,' groaned Dell desperately. 'Look. I'm a rich man, a businessman. Help me and you won't be sorry.'

He looked appealingly at the uniformed guard. 'Video-phone my factory will you? Contact my partner, Bender's his name, and tell him to send a car for me. The number is Central City 2453.'

'So you're a businessman are you?' The guard spat with undisguised disgust and tightened his grip on the long club. 'A fine sort of a fool I'd look spending my money on a long-distance videophone call. You gutter scum are all alike, now get up and get out before I finish what someone else started.'

'Long distance?' Dell stared at the grim-faced guard.

'What are you talking about? I'll give you a hundred times what the call would cost.' He stared a little desperately at the guard. 'Look. You must have heard of me. Weston, Dell Weston, I own a factory in the city, I manufacture cocaine. You must have heard of me.'

'I haven't,' snapped the guard curtly. 'I don't know what you think you're doing, but maybe that smack on the head has spoiled your wits. I've never heard of any Dell Weston, and Central City is over two-thousand miles from here, now get out and stay out!'

Impatiently he gripped Dell by the shoulder and dragged him to his feet. He pushed, gesturing with the long club towards a narrow alley. 'Get out of this area. If I find you in here again I'll split your skull. Move!'

Numbly Dell moved towards the

mouth of the narrow alley. He staggered a little and the throbbing wound on the side of his head sent stabs of agony lancing through his brain. He paused, glancing back at the busy yards behind, at the sweating men loading trucks with bales and boxes beneath the brilliant white glare of arc lights, and at the watching figure of the uniformed guard.

He could expect nothing but suspicion here.

Painfully he forced himself towards the alley, obviously one of the boundaries of the guarded area. Here the lights were dim and the sound of busy men faded to a low murmur, like the drone of distant machinery. He rested his aching body against a rough brick wall, pressing his forehead against the cold wet surface, and forced himself to think.

He was in trouble.

A stranger in a strange city. An object of suspicion, without friends, without money, without any means of contacting the one man who could help him. Or would he?

The rain almost numbed him with its

cold drizzle but it helped clear his throbbing senses. Desperately he examined the tattered rags covering his shivering body, the pockets were empty, devoid of even a single coin or scrap of paper. His forehead felt sore and the taste in his mouth could only have come from drugs.

Someone had beaten him senseless, kept him unconscious with narcotics, and then had transported him to a city two thousand miles from where he was known. Who?

He thought that he knew.

Bender was the only one who stood to gain by such an action. Thugs wouldn't have drugged him, they would have left his dead or stunned figure in the alley, certainly they wouldn't have troubled either to change his clothes or transport him so far. His partner must have done it. Dell could guess why.

His dead body in the city would have aroused curiosity and Bender would have run the risk of being accused of breaking the Ethical Contract. Even if this had been overcome, yet their relationship would have stopped the man from actually causing his death. There was a queer streak of distorted logic in the man. Something within him hesitated a the grim finality of killing the man he hated, and so, while he could order his assassins to beat him, rob and strand him, yet he could convince himself that he had not actually killed him.

Sweat oozed in great beads from his forehead as he rested against the wet, cold brick of the wall. He breathed in great rasping gulps and the muscles of his legs and thighs tensed and quivered beneath the stress of a rage so intense and savage as to almost drain the blood from his spinning brain.

Bender had done this! Bender had robbed him, stranded him, put him in immediate danger of losing his life. His own partner had done it, done it for the stream of wealth that would inevitably result from this unrestricted flow of cocaine. He had both the Arbitrator's opinion and the recorded agreement for all-out production, and Dell would have only been a hindrance.

Bender had done all this, and he had done something else.

He had killed Madge!

The assassin hadn't missed. His target had been the woman, not the man. While Madge remained alive to ask awkward questions Bender had to move carefully. He knew Madge too well to ever hope to gain full control while she claimed title to half the profits, and so she had died.

Dell leaned against the rough wall and fought for self-control. His lips thinned as he thought of what must have happened, and his hands clenched as he imagined what he would do to his partner if ever he had the chance. Slowly sanity returned, the awareness of where he was and the position he was in, and stiffly he straightened from the wall and moved towards the flaring lights of the city.

A bitter wind had risen, driving the freezing rain like barbs against his naked flesh, and shuddering with the cold he tried to gather his rags closer around him. The narrow alley appeared deserted, but he had the sensation of eyes watching him and once a man stepped from a shadowed doorway, staring at him, then muttering a curse as he saw the tattered rags.

Dell grinned without humour. Even the gutter rats didn't consider him worth robbing. He staggered a little as he entered the brightly lit pleasure section of the city. A few cars whined along the streets, their turbines shrilling as they slowed before the warm-looking entrances of restaurants and nightclubs, disgorging well-dressed men and women, attended by their watchful guards and stared at by a little huddle of beggars.

A man lurched along the street, a medium-built man with a scowling face and angry eyes. Dell stepped before him, one hand outstretched.

'Wait.'

'Well?'

'I'm a stranger here, could you direct me to the charity wards?'

'Charity wards?' The man laughed and stared at Dell with hard eyes. 'You must be a stranger, we don't believe in charity here.'

'Then could you help me? I need a meal and somewhere warm to sleep.

Please, if you could just tell me where to go I'd be grateful.'

'To hell,' said the man and roared with ugly amusement. 'They tell me it's warm there, and the dead don't need to eat.'

'Please,' insisted Dell desperately. 'I'm sick, I need warmth and food.'

'So do I,' snarled the man. 'So do we all. Who are you to get what my wife died for want of, my children starved for? Who are you I say?'

He stepped forward, peering into Dell's face.

'So you're one of them are you?' He raised his hand and Dell reeled to the impact of the savage blow. 'Get away from me you gutter rat, get away before I kick your ribs in.'

'Wait,' gasped Dell. 'I'll pay you. I'll pay you a thousand times if you will only help me now. I . . . '

He stepped back as the man lunged forward, the intent to murder naked and ugly in his hard eyes. For one moment he tried to reason with the man, then better sense and nature prevailed, and his feet slipped on the frozen rain as he ran.

Laughter rang after him, strained and hysterical, hopeless and bitter, echoing from the blind faces of the looming buildings and whispering along the winding street, but the man did not follow and soon he was beyond the insane sound.

Dell rested against a building, feeling his feet and legs grow numb with the intense cold and feeling the shivering sweat of incipient fever begin to take hold. He had to get warmth and food. Had to. Unless he found shelter he would die, and he had to find it soon.

He stared at the bright front of a low-class dining room, and straightened with sudden hope. Such places weren't too particular, and if they'd let him wash dishes he would be in the warm and could probably earn the price of a meal.

Quickly he crossed the street and thrust at the swing doors.

Heat laved him from within the dingy place, an odorous warmth composed of cooking smells, stale air, smoke and human sweat, but it was warm and he relaxed for a moment letting the chill thaw from his feet and legs. A man glared at him from behind a counter and a corpulent guard shifted on a stool watching him with little bloodshot eyes.

'What you want?'

'Please,' said Dell to the man behind the counter. 'I'm broke. Will you let me work off the price of a meal?'

The man grunted, studying him with shrewd, thoughtful eyes and glanced at something beyond Dell's range of vision.

'Broke are you?'

'Yes.'

'Not too particular how you earn a little cash?'

'No,' said Dell, and felt his stomach churn as he guessed what was coming.

'You look a big man, a fighting man, tell you what I'll do.' The man leaned confidently over the counter. 'I'll stake you to a meal if you'll fight one of my boys.'

'Bare fists?'

'Hell no, we want something more exciting than that. Knives, and if you win I'll give you ten credits and the chance to fight again. How about it?'

Dell shuddered and tried not to show his distaste. He had heard of these knife fights, reminiscent of the old gladiatorial combats in the arenas of ancient Rome, though he had never seen one. Men were stripped to the waist and armed with ten-inch knives, then faced each other in a roped circle. Sometimes they fought to the death, but more often it was until one or both were so badly slashed that they collapsed from loss of blood or exhaustion. It was a sport designed to appeal to jaded emotions, to the bloodlust inherent in mankind, and it flourished in the poorer sections of the cities.

'Well?' The man stared at him and jerked his head at the guard. 'A free meal and a chance of ten credits, do you want it?'

'I'm sick,' muttered Dell. 'All I want is a meal, I'm in no condition for fighting.'

'Outside,' ordered the guard. He rose from his stool and reached for his long club.

'Wait a minute,' said the man behind the counter. 'Maybe he'll feel different after a meal.' He turned to Dell again. 'It won't be too bad, just a few cuts, and if you're fast not even that. The boy I've got to match you is a hop-head, you'd win sure. Think it over.'

'No. No I can't.' Dell stared miserably at the man, reluctant to leave the warmth of the dining room.

'You're a fool,' said the man calmly. He reached down behind the counter and produced a squat bottle. 'Maybe you'd feel better after a drink?'

'Why waste that stuff on him,' snapped the guard. 'Kick him out.'

'Shut up, it's my stuff and I'll give it to whom I like.'

'You're wasting your time, look at him, scared yellow.'

'Are you?' The man stared at Dell. 'Scared I mean?' He leaned a little closer. 'Look,' he said urgently. 'I'm in a spot. My customers are expecting a fight and if they don't get it I'll lose trade. How about it? A free meal, ten credits certain and twenty if you win.'

'Sorry,' said Dell. 'I'm no fighter, I wouldn't even give them a show. All I want is the chance to work, do I get it?'

'Not here,' snapped the man angrily. He jerked his thumb towards the door. 'You've had your chance, now get outside.'

Dell didn't move. He stood staring hopefully at the man, not daring to leave the warmth for the freezing death waiting outside. The guard grinned and reached for his club, rising slowly from his stool.

'You heard,' he said gently. 'Outside!'

'Please,' said Dell urgently. 'Give me some work, anything, if I go outside now I'll be going to my death. I'm sick I tell you, sick.'

He stared at them, knowing that it was hopeless to appeal to their charity, knowing that he either fought as the owner wanted or would be beaten senseless by the guard. He licked his lips, shivering at the touch of fever, then gulped and thrust through the swing doors.

The wind slashed at him like a knife!

It was freezing hard now, the rain had stopped and the wetness on the street had turned to ice. Lights shone with a harsh glare from arc lights suspended above, and a few huddled figures hunched together for warmth clustered outside the few nightclubs and restaurants.

Beggars, and he was one of them.

A man stared at him and spat. A woman looked at him and shrilled a curse. A guard laughed and swung his club, and both men and women sniggered as he scurried away. They wouldn't even let him become a beggar.

He leaned against a blank shop front, and fought for rationalisation. Something was wrong, something was terribly wrong. A man had all the freedom he wanted or could use. He could become a beggar and no one would object, but they had, and Dell wondered why.

Staring into the metal shuttered window he found his answer.

A debtor's brand!

7

He stood for a long time, leaning against the blank window and staring at his reflection in the polished steel of the shutter. His throat had constricted until it was hard to breathe and his heart thudded against his ribs with a force that seemed to shake his entire body.

Now he knew!

Now he realised why even the beggars hated him, why the man he had accosted had threatened him, why the dining room owner had offered him what he had. A debtor. A pariah, scum, outcast and unwanted. A thing to be despised and kicked, used and tossed aside, a scrap of human debris hovering on the thin edge of annihilation.

Slowly he raised his hand and rubbed at the writhing brand on his forehead. It wasn't stain, it wasn't a dye which would fade with the passing of time. The brand had been tattooed into the flesh and it would remain with him until the day of his death, and as he felt the bitter lash of the freezing night wind, he knew that death was already too close.

He had to find shelter!

A man passed close to the edge of the street, a tall man reeling a little and with his eyes glazed with the drug-induced euphoria of marijuana. Dell stared at him, fighting down the lingering shreds of moral reluctance. There was no crime in this world, and what he intended was neither criminally nor morally wrong, but he still didn't like it.

He followed the man, breathing in great gasps as he forced himself to remain calm and by oxygenating his blood, hoping to ease his overstrained nerves. A patch of deep shadow loomed ahead and for a moment he thought that his quarry would avoid it, and despite his misery half hoped that what he intended would be rendered impossible.

The man hesitated, then shrugged and strode into the shadows. Dell slipped after him, his lips pressed hard against his teeth and his body sweating with anticipated effort. Three long running steps and he was just behind the man. One more and he raised his fist, grabbed at the half-seen shoulder before him, twisted, struck — and missed!

Something smashed into his face, sending little flashes of light exploding in his brain and filling his mouth with the warm saltiness of blood. Desperately he twisted away: from a second blow, slipping on ice and running down the street away from his intended victim.

He sobbed as he ran, sobbed with pain and despair, his shoulders twitching in anticipation of a high-velocity bullet. What he had done merited death, not because he had tried to rob a man, but because he had failed and he made a perfect target against the white glare of the arc lights.

Luck was with him. Either the man wasn't armed or he didn't want to waste ammunition, but no shot came and after running for half a mile Dell staggered into a doorway and slumped against the barred panel.

He felt physically and mentally sick.

His problem was a simple one — to stay alive. He knew it, and knew that unless he could manage to find shelter for the night he was as good as dead. He could beg — but the other beggars wouldn't tolerate him near them. He could steal — but he was a stranger and didn't know the city, any attempt at theft would result in certain death. He could rob — but lacked both physical strength and the savage indifference essential to a thug. He was a businessman, not a scavenger. He had grown too accustomed to shielding guards, soft living, easy wealth. He had forgotten what the lower levels of civilisation were really like, and unless he learned and learned fast he would never see the dawn.

It was as simple as that.

He smiled a little, his lips thinning against his teeth, and deliberately flexed the muscles of fingers and wrists. He couldn't attack an unsuspecting man, but he could still fight an armed adversary and win or lose his problem would be solved.

Stiffly he climbed to his feet and

headed back towards the centre of the city.

The dining room was still filled with odorous warmth, the guard dozed as he slumped on his stool, and the man behind the counter scowled as he swabbed the stained plastic. He glanced up as Dell entered and flung down the filthy cloth.

'So it's you again.'

'Yes,' said Dell. He ignored the sadistic stare of the alerted guard, and rested his hands on the edge of the counter. 'I could use that drink now.'

'You mean . . . ?' The man stared at him and reached for the bottle. He poised it over a cracked glass and looked suspiciously at the man before him.

'If this is a try-on for a free drink you'll be sorry.' He jerked his head at the guard and the man grunted as he rose from the stool and stood in front of the door. 'If it is you'll be shot down before you take three steps. Well?'

'Give me the drink,' snapped Dell. He tried to still the quivering of his hands as he reached for the thick glass and felt the alcohol sear his throat and fill his shivering body with welcome heat. 'Where's the food?'

'You're going to fight?' The man poised the bottle again. 'Remember what I said? Ten credits certain and twenty if you win?'

'I remember.' Dell swallowed the second drink. 'Money first, if I lose you can take it off me, if I win I stay here the night. Agreed?'

'Sure.' The man yelled something into a hatch behind him, then looked at Dell with a strange expression. 'Have another drink?'

'No, and just in case you've any bright ideas, remember that you and I have an Ethical Contract, don't break it.'

'The hell with that,' snapped the man. 'Who's to know?'

'No one, but maybe a clear conscience is worth a little more than a few credits, and the guard will know.'

'That souse?' The man laughed, and sneered at the piggy-eyed guard. 'A bottle would keep him quiet for the rest of his life.'

'Perhaps, and then perhaps he might

think that once you've broken the contract there'd be nothing to stop him killing you and helping himself.' Dell grinned at the startled expression on the man's face. 'Think it over.'

'I will,' promised the man, and reaching into the hatch put a great bowl of steaming stew on the counter. 'Eat now, you fight in thirty minutes.'

Dell nodded and reached for a spoon.

The food was thick with grease and redolent of the scrapings from a thousand plates, but it was hot and nourishing and it tasted wonderful. Dell gulped hungrily at it, almost amused at what he would have thought of the mess a few hours ago, then forcing himself to forget the past in the nearing peril of the future.

He had to fight.

There was no way out of it, not now. Not after he had taken the drinks and eaten the food. Like it or not he was going to face an armed man and the battle would be quick and savage and probably lethal. It would be quick because he doubted his strength, savage because each would know that mercy was a thing unknown and unexpected. Lethal because ten-inch knives weren't toys and a lucky thrust could end the fight with fortunate speed.

He felt surprisingly calm.

It lasted while he stripped off the rags covering his upper body, while he examined the needle-pointed, razor-edged knife, while he moved like a thing of wood towards the back room, the ring and the waiting crowd. It lasted until he stepped into the roped circle with the glare of arc lights blazing down from above and an unseen sea of eyes glittering at him from the surrounding darkness.

Then he saw his opponent and he felt sudden terror.

This was no hop-head, no boy, no callow gutter rat trying to earn the price of a meal. He was small and slender, lithe and feral-eyed, his muscular torso bore the thin white traces of many scars and he gripped the glittering weapon with practised ease. A knife-fighter! A professional! A born killer — and Dell was his next victim.

He slipped into the circle, a thin grin

wreathing his savage mouth and his glittering eyes staring with sadistic hunger at the middle-aged man before him. He turned to the hidden crowd, waving the knife and smiling at the roar of approval echoing from the smoke-filled room, then turned and stared at Dell with an expression of cold calculation.

Like a butcher, thought Dell sickly. An artist judging just how long he could drag out the torment of gaping wounds and severed tendons. A showman, catering to the blood-lust of the hidden audience, and determined to give them value for their money. He moved across the ring and Dell shuddered as he noticed the cat-like stride, the sure-footed approach. He halted in the centre of the cleared space, knife extended before him, and automatically Dell moved towards him.

Their knives clashed, the metal ringing as the blades touched, and a man slipped into the ring beside them.

'At the sound of the bell retreat to opposite sides of the ring. At the sound of the second bell come out fighting. No rests, no rounds, the last man on his feet wins. Understand?'

'Yes,' said Dell tensely. He could hardly force himself to speak.

'Yeah,' grunted the slender man indifferently. He grinned, showing mouthful of rotten teeth and the thin white scar-lines writhed on his naked torso. 'Don't worry, pal,' he muttered reassuringly. 'I won't hurt you — much!'

He laughed slapping the blade of his knife against that of Dell's, then spun as the bell rang and rested easily against the ropes. Opposite him Dell tried to rid himself of his paralysing fear, forcing himself to be calm and feeling sweat ooze from his forehead and palms in great chilly drops.

He held the glittering blade of the knife before and a little to the right, thumb to the blade and the edge pointing towards his left. That way he could cut either up or down, stab, rip forehand or backhand, and at the same time use the knife to parry any attack. He knew the theory of knife fighting — but knowing the theory and having the experience were two entirely different things.

The bell rang again, and the slender man dissolved in a blur of motion.

He writhed across the ring, sprang to one side, returned, feinted with his knife, lunged, twisted — and darted away. Dell heard the savage roar from the crowd, felt a thin line of fire trace itself across his ribs, and stared down at a long shallow cut on his chest. He felt foolish, still in almost the same position as he had stood at the sound of the bell, the knife in his hand and blood rilling from his wound.

He didn't have a chance!

The man was quick, too quick. He trod lithely around the slow-moving figure of the middle-aged man his lips curved in. a smile of careless anticipation. He would make this one last. A clever succession of cuts criss-crossing the torso, back and arms. Some expert knife play with the edge and plenty of blood. A pity the man was so slow, these gutter rats made poor opponents, but they were safe and he could always play to the grandstand. The audience expected a good fight, they always expected that, and it was the audience that kept him in business.

He moved closer, the brilliant illumination sparkling from the polished steel in his hand, and Deli watched him as a rabbit might watch a snake.

Fear gripped him. A deadly soul-destroying fear. A horror of the glittering knife before him, a cringing from the razor-edged steel. He wanted to run, to escape into the freezing wind outside, to hide in the darkness and cower alone and safe in some hidden place. He sweated with fear, trembled with panic, shook with utter dread.

And then came the calmness of desperation.

He had nothing to lose. Nothing. No matter what he did things couldn't be worse than what they were. He could die fighting, or he could stand and make a Roman holiday for the blood-hungry audience. If he just stood and waited for slow death it would be no worse than a sudden thrust. One way he would be butchered, the other . . .

He gritted his teeth, and sprang heavily aside from a slashing cut. He whirled,

parrying with his knife, trying to antici-
pate the next move. Something stung his
arm, something else stung his side, blood
rilled down his body, soaking into the top
of his trousers, mingling with sweat and
painting his body an ugly red.

Again the slender man danced away,
his knife dulled a little now, the bright
steel mottled with red stains. He wiped
the blade against the side of his leg, and
grinned contemptuously at Dell's clumsy
movements.

'Come on,' he jeered. 'Move about a
bit, it will keep you warm.'

Dell grunted, saving his breath, and as
the slender man weaved closer, lunged
forward, bringing up his knife in a ripping
cut.

He missed. He had known that he
would miss, but as the lithe figure before
him spun away from the threatening
blade he struck with the clenched fist of
his left hand, and grinned with savage
enjoyment as cartilage pulped beneath his
blow.

Quickly he twisted, bringing back his
knife in a wide circle, the edge towards

his left and the point outwards. It struck something soft and jubilantly he dragged the blade towards him, feeling flesh cringe and recoil from the slashing cut, then sprang away and stood poised on the balls of his feet as he faced his opponent

The slender man screamed!

He stared at Dell, his eyes a glittering hell as they stared from above his pulped nose. Blood rilled down his face, mingling with the red trickle from the deep cut in his side. He trembled, quivering with sheer insane rage and pain, then gulped and moved relentlessly forward.

'You . . . ' He spat and dragged the back of his hand across his ruined features. 'I was going to be gentle with you, treat you easy, cut you up a bit and let you drop after a while. Alive and not too badly hurt, but now . . . '

He whispered what he intended doing, the sound of his voice a rasping snarl as he described how Dell would look and feel after the knife had ripped his stomach, slashed his face to ribbons, stabbed at nerves and turned his body into a jangling hell of unbelievable torment.

Listening made Dell feel sick. He felt the return of paralysing fear and fought desperately for self-control. Once he let the man scare him, chill his blood and slow his reactions, it would be over. He would die beneath the flashing blade of the other's weapon, a thing of horror, a tormented wreck of what had once been a man, and he knew that after his blow he could expect no mercy.

The slender man weaved closer, running his tongue over his swollen lips, the light in his eyes matched by the glitter of cold steel in his hand. He moved like a dancer or an old-time fighter, balanced on his toes, ready to leap in any direction or attack from any angle.

Dell stepped to one side, lunged forward and jerked back as steel hissed towards his stomach. Frantically he parried a slash at his face, the knives clicking together oddly loud in the tense silence, and twisted as a knee thrust towards his groin.

He caught the blow on the side of his thigh, and while the slender man was off balance, pushed and cut at a sweat-marked torso. Blood followed the path of his blade, and he felt a surge of triumph and stepped closer for a second attack. Steel burned his arm, a searing white-hot agony as the knife buried itself three inches deep into the bicep and the pain brought sudden caution.

He jerked away, half-running towards the centre of the ring and stood watching as the slender man wiped blood from the long shallow gash across his chest.

It couldn't last.

He was an amateur, a middle-aged man against a trained fighter and he didn't stand a chance. So far his opponent had been playing with him, making a show for the audience and taking his time, but anger and the pain of his broken nose had turned him savage and the next attack would be the last.

Dell watched the man as he weaved across the ring studying the flashing eyes, the glittering blade of the knife, the contemptuous smile on the swollen lips. Against this man he was slow and helpless, meat for the slaughter, but he had one desperate chance.

He steadied himself on the balls of his feet, shifting his grip on the hilt of the knife and gauging the distance between them with desperate intensity. He tensed, half-turned, lifted his arm — and threw the knife.

It was unexpected, startling, the one thing no knife-fighter ever did, for it disarmed the thrower, and so it was the one thing unguarded against. The slender man coughed, stared stupidly down at the knife buried in his chest, then he fell, a red flood gushing from between his sneering lips.

It was over.

8

Dawn came with a thin sleet and a bleak light. Sullen clouds hid the distant sun, scudding over the heavens like a pall of lead, like a grey inverted sea, like the ashes of dead and forgotten dreams, bitter and colourless, fitting accompaniment to the world below.

Dell sat at a small table in the dining room, sipping at scalding coffee, and trying to forget the burning pain of his wounds. The owner had coated them with a clear plastic dressing, a sterile antiseptic that hardened to a flexible dressing, but beneath the transparent film they itched and burned with nerve-rasping torment.

He had eaten again, slept a little, and the money in his pockets felt good to the touch. The audience had appreciated the battle and they had signalled their enjoyment at the surprise ending in the usual way. Dell had picked up more than fifty credits from the blood-smeared ring, and with the twenty from the owner he felt a new man.

He drained the cup and relaxed, savouring the moist warmth of the eating place and staving off the necessity of making a move.

'Finished?' The owner slipped into a seat across the table and fumbled for a limp package of cigarettes. He lit one, and the sickly scent of marijuana coiled between them.

'Yes.'

'Decided yet?'

'I'm not going to fight again if that's what you mean, once was enough.'

'Maybe you're right,' agreed the man. He drew on the loosely rolled cigarette, inhaling the acrid smoke and letting it stream in twin plumes from his nostrils. 'That trick of throwing the blade wouldn't work again.' He looked at Dell with reluctant admiration.

'Man but you were lucky! I never thought that you'd last ten minutes, and when you smashed his nose I was certain of it. What made you try a throw?'

Dell shrugged.

'Desperation perhaps, I had nothing to lose and I was lucky. He just didn't expect it.'

'Suppose you had missed? Just wounded him a little, and stood unarmed, what would you have done then?'

'What could I have done?' Dell grinned, then winced at a stab of pain from his wounded arm. 'Let's forget it shall we?'

'As you say, but I wish that you'd fight again, good men aren't too easy to get, not with what I can afford to pay them.'

He looked up as the door swung open, then jerked the cigarette from his mouth and sprang to his feet.

A girl stood just within the doorway.

She was young, and yet her eyes had the hardness of those who have seen too much of the bitter side of life. Dark hair piled in a thick plait around her head, a coronet-like coil of gleaming black tresses. Her features were small and surprisingly delicate with a full soft mouth and long slender neck, but her mouth was firm, and faint lines had traced their imprint of worry and suffering around the soft lips.

She stood, hugging a ragged cloak close around her lithe figure, and Dell half-rose from his chair as the owner stepped before her.

'You again. What do you want?'

'You know what I want,' she said, and her voice was deep and startlingly musical. 'Food. Scraps from your kitchen, scrapings from your dirty plates. Anything edible.'

'I've nothing for you. Get out!'

'Wait!' Dell rose from his chair and stepped beside the woman. 'Are you hungry?'

'Need you ask?' She stared at him with wide calculating eyes, noting the brand on his forehead and the stiffness with which he moved. A tiny frown furrowed her arched brows and she moved a little from him.

'Don't be afraid,' said Dell reassuringly. 'I'm harmless.' He gripped her arm and steered her towards the table. She resisted for a moment, then shrugged and sat down opposite him. The owner glowered at them, and irritably slammed the door.

'Two coffees,' ordered Dell. 'Big and

hot, and bring some food.'

'Are you insane?' The man glared at Dell then at the slight figure of the woman. 'What are you wasting your money on this beggar for?'

'It's my money,' said Dell quietly. 'Do we get the food or do we go somewhere else?'

'I still think that you're insane, she's an Anti.'

'She is hungry, and I'm getting impatient. Are you going to serve us or not?'

The owner scowled, then yelled something down a hatch.

He returned with two big mugs of coffee and plates of steaming food. He slammed them down onto the table, then sat on a stool behind the counter, lighting a fresh cigarette, and staring sombrely at the rain-lashed dawn beyond the dirty windows.

Dell sipped at his coffee, picked up his knife and fork, smiled at the girl and began to eat. She hesitated a moment, then with a muffled sob began to tear at her food, cramming her mouth and eating with a feral hunger unpleasant to see in one so young.

For a while they ate in silence, enjoying the food, stale and musty though it was, not knowing when or where they would eat again.

Dell sighed, pushing away his empty plate and gulping the last of his coffee.

'Want to talk?'

She looked at him, and again he felt her eyes drift to the ugly brand tattooed on his forehead, then lower until she stared at his features.

'Who are you?'

'Does it matter?' Dell shrugged and gestured towards his forehead. 'I carry what I am for all to see. Does it shock you?'

'No.' She lowered her gaze, flushing a little and picking idly at the handle of her cup. 'Why did you buy me food?'

'Why not? You were hungry, I have money, what more natural than I should buy you a meal?'

'Was that the only reason?'

He stared at her, then as her meaning registered, turned scarlet and glanced away.

'That was the only reason,' he said quietly. 'I intended nothing else. Do you believe me?'

'Yes.' Impulsively she gripped his arm and he flinched from the pressure against his wound.

'You're hurt!'

'It's nothing.' He smiled a little ruefully and touched his throbbing arm. 'A scratch, forget it.'

'You fought last night, didn't you?' She glanced towards the silent owner crouched on his stool. 'I know what happened in the back room; we all know. Did you win?'

'Need you ask?'

'No. The fact that you're alive proves that you must have won.' She stared at him again, searching his features with her wide blue eyes. 'You're not a fighter, you're not even a debtor, who are you?'

'Weston. Dell Weston, one-time businessman from Central City, two-thousand miles from here.'

'Two-thousand miles?' She frowned. 'But, Dell, Central City isn't more than two-hundred miles away. What made you think it was so far?'

'Two-hundred!' He stared at her, then relaxed, smiling bitterly as he remembered the events of the past few hours. 'Now I understand. That guard must have been paid to watch me, to drive me into the city before I could learn too much.' He grinned at her puzzled expression. 'Sorry, I'd forgotten that you didn't know about that. Now it's your turn. Who are you?'

'An Anti.' She flushed a little at his expression. 'I'm not ashamed of it, and I wasn't begging for myself, we are trying to establish a charity ward here, soup for the starving and shelter for the homeless.'

'I know what you mean,' said Dell. 'We have one in Central City, but I didn't mean that. What is your name?'

'Lorna. Lorna Freniss. Free, white and over twenty-one. An Anti from choice, and proud of it!'

'Why not?' Dell toyed with his empty cup and tried not to ask the questions bubbling within him. Lorna smiled and gently touched his hand.

'We have a lot in common you and I, Dell. You don't really like the world the way it is do you? I know that you never deserved that brand, it's too recent and you haven't starved long enough, your face hasn't the bleak look you get when you've worried too long and hungered too often. You're like all the others, caught up in something too strong for you, or rather too foul for you to enter into. You are a decent man, Dell, really decent, and don't you think that it's time you did something about it?'

'Do something about it?' He stared at her, frowning and trying to catch her inner meaning. 'Do what?'

'Join us, Dell. Join the Antis. Help us to restore a little law and order in the world.'

He had expected it. He had known it was coming from the first moment, and yet still he didn't know what to do. This was a free world, a really free world, and any attempt to impose regulation and penalty-enforced law would meet with violent and savage opposition. The Antis fought a lost cause, a hopeless dream of reviving something long dead, and yet . . . ?

It would be good to walk without a gun or an armed guard, secure in the knowledge that he was safe from attack. It would be good to prevent men drugging themselves into beasts. To end the thin faces and emaciated bodies of beggar children, and the pitiful huddle of starving homeless. He wondered what it would be like to live in a world free of fear, the eternal fear of jungle law, the horrible fear of the weak and helpless.

A part of him knew that he sought justification for his own failure, but he crushed the feeling, imagining a world in which men knew what they did and what their neighbours did, knowing that their actions were controlled by law.

And yet . . . ?

The Arbitrator had talked with cold logic, and what he had said made sense. No race could be more free than an individual of that race. Enslave one, and you enslaved all.

'Worried about it?' Lorna leaned a little nearer, bending forward across the table and lowering her voice. 'You were a businessman you said, how did it feel knowing that every man who had a gun was trying to steal what you owned? How did you like waking in the morning and worrying whether or not you still had a factory? Did you like having to hire armed guards to protect your property, more guards to protect your life? Ask the owner of this place how he likes living on his nerves, trying to do without sleep because he can't afford full-time protection, and having to promote knife fights to attract customers. Do you think that he enjoys life? If you do just look at him and think again.'

Dell glanced to where the owner sat on his stool, acrid smoke coiling from the marijuana cigarette between his lips, and his eyes dull and lifeless as they stared at the grey dawn.

Lorna was right.

The struggle was too much, too strenuous, too savage. A man had to think of too many things, and it drained his energies and sapped his strength. Business was a nightmare, a juggling with human relationships and forced demands. A tightrope, where a single slip meant poverty and degradation. He thought of the brand on his forehead, and shuddered. If to be a businessman was bad, to be a pauper was . . .

Hell.

No one wanted the man who had nothing. No one would give a meal or a single coin to someone who could never repay. Life was too hard for charity, too tough for sentiment. To be generous was to be a fool, and to have nothing was to live on the thin edge of extinction.

Such a man had nothing to lose.

He opened his lips to agree, then hesitated again as he remembered the calm tones of the Arbitrator. The man had spoken with conviction, and Dell was intelligent enough to know that it was useless railing against a system when he himself could be at fault. Like any other man of his age he had a healthy contempt for those who blamed anything and everything but themselves, and the thought acted like a cold douche on his smouldering rebellion.

'You may be right, Lorna,' he said quietly. 'I agree that things could be better, but is penalty-enforced law the only way?'

'Can you think of another?' She stared at him, her wide, dark eyes burning with idealistic conviction. 'Who will help us if we can't help ourselves? Would you permit your children to play with fire? I tell you, Dell, that mankind isn't ready for anarchy, human nature is too near that of the jungle, too beast-like. We can't control ourselves, we need the weight of tradition and elected Authority. We need a set of rules to live by and unless we get them Earth will be a chaos within two generations!'

'I still don't see it.' Dell stirred uncomfortably in his chair, trying to ease the pain of his throbbing wounds. He felt tired, and his eyes stung as if they were filled with sharp sand. 'We're adult people, not children, and unless one is free then none are. Naturally this is a time of adjustment, a period of flux and change, but perhaps it will all settle itself without the Antis.'

'How?' She smiled bitterly, her full lips curving with scorn. 'When we are all stupid drug addicts, made so by power seekers and greedy mannfacturers? When our streets are littered with dead and we have forgotten what it is to be able to trust our nearest friends? When transportation slows for lack of fuel and people desert the cities for lack of food? When will the new era dawn, Dell? When?'

He stirred again, wishing that she had never started the conversation. It was hard to think. His stomach writhed with nausea and his head throbbed with a dull ache caused by over-exertion and lack of rest. Even if she were right. and he still had his doubts, what could they do? He knew a little of the Antis, they established charity wards, preached on street corners, and railed against everything and everybody. Fanatics the lot of them, and yet . . . ?

Could they be right?

'I still don't know,' he said a little shamefacedly. 'The Arbitrator spoke as well as you do, and he made just as good a case for utter personal freedom. Who is right, you or they?'

'The Arbitrators?' Loma stared at him, her face white and strained. 'You have spoken to them?'

'We called in one to settle a dispute, I lost the opinion, but what he said stuck in my mind.' He stared a little helplessly around the dingy dining room. 'You see, Lorna, we have no standards of comparison, we don't realise just what is was like in the old days. How can we be certain: that penalty-enforced rule would be any better than utter freedom?'

'So you've spoken with an Arbitrator.' Lorna didn't appear to have heard what he had said. 'You've listened to one, taken his advice, let him rule you.' She stared at Dell, little spots of colour flaming high on her pale cheeks

'You fool!'

'Why, Lorna? Why?'

'Because they started all this,' she said bitterly. 'That's why!'

He stared at her in shocked disbelief.

9

The day wore on, and as the light grew so did the life of the city. Turbine cars whined as they darted along the streets, carrying businessmen with their guards, a few workers late for their employment, and a scattering of the leisured classes returning home from their night's pleasure.

The crowds of beggars had scattered, gone on their eternal rounds of the garbage bins or slinking to some hole for a brief rest. Guards relieved each other, the weary-faced night shift giving place to the day. Shops opened, factories, restaurants, the little kiosks selling three kinds of cigarettes and tiny bundles of dope. Men stopped at them, women too, pasty-faced and twitching as they impatiently waited for the drugs which would give them courage to face another day. They tossed down hard-earned coins and snatched their purchases, hurrying on with bright eyes and flushed faces.

Dell stared at them, trying not to feel contempt, but unable to feel pity. Lorna tugged at his sleeve.

'Come on, Dell. We haven't got all day.'

'Wait,' he said, reluctant to move. The sight of the wakening city interested him, and now he examined it with new eyes, the eyes of one apart. The brand on his forehead made him that, an outsider, he could have no part of normal life while he wore it.

'You didn't believe me when I told you that the Arbitrators had caused all this.' Lorna tugged at his arm again. 'Are you afraid to have me prove it?'

'Can you?' He sighed a little and allowed her to guide him along the unfamiliar streets. 'How could they?'

'They did, that's all I know, and that is enough.' She glanced at him, tilting her head to stare upwards at his set features. 'You still don't believe me do you?'

'No.'

'I thought not. Well, I'm taking you to someone who will convince you.'

'Who?'

'Does that matter?' She smiled up at him as she steered him between a maze of narrow alleys. He stared down at her, his eyes hard.

'It might. You could have fixed something like this just to aid recruiting, come to think of it you probably have.'

'Suspicious, aren't you?'

'I've reason to be,' he said grimly. He gestured towards his forehead. 'That came of being careless, of trusting someone too far. I don't intend to let it happen again.'

She shrugged, and they walked through the narrow streets in silence and mounting suspicion.

A warehouse loomed before them, a gaunt, tumbledown structure of boarded windows and blank walls. The roof sagged a little, and the place reeked of damp and decay. It had a hangdog look, like a building that had seen better days and couldn't forget it.

A door looked like a scabbed wound in one wall, a paintless collection of half-rotted boards, strapped with bars of rusted metal and with a judas window.

Lorna rapped on the bare wood, three short and two long. She waited for five seconds, then rapped again, reversing the signal. Metal grated and the grill window slid to one side. A man stared at them, his eyes shining like those of some animal as he peered from the darkness.

'Yes?'

'You know me,' she snapped impatiently. 'Let me in.'

'Who's your friend?'

'Dell Weston. Never mind him, open up.'

The man grunted and slammed the tiny window. Metal scraped and slowly the door swung wide. Lorna gripped Dell's arm, and together they entered the dank building.

'The Professor in?'

'Upstairs,' grunted the man. 'You know the way.' He slammed and locked the door, slumping down on a hard stool and fumbling with tobacco as he rolled a loose cigarette.

Lorna ignored him, and jerking her head at Dell headed for a flight of dilapidated stairs. He hesitated a moment, looking at the doorman, noting the red brand on the man's forehead, then he shrugged.

Beggars couldn't be choosers.

A man rose from a cot as they entered the upstairs room, an old man, white-haired and thin-faced, with trembling hands and eyes that seemed to hold all the bitterness of the world. He brushed at his rags as he saw the woman, running thin, dirty fingers through his mane of hair, and making a pitiful effort to remember his dignity. Dell stared at him, then at the room in which the man obviously slept.

And received his first surprise.

It was a laboratory, a combination of makeshift benches and modern equipment. A small generator stood in one corner and ranked instruments studded irregular panels of grey slate. It was a combination of sleek perfection and rough workmanship, a welding of primitive and ultra-modern. Looking at it. Dell felt a new and unfamiliar respect for the thin-faced old man and the slender bodied woman.

'Did you build all this?'

'Some of it,' said the man. 'We improvised what we couldn't beg or steal, and fortunately we found a backer.'

'Carter,' said the woman warningly, 'be careful!'

'It doesn't matter,' assured Dell. He glanced again at the equipment. 'If you can prove that what you say is true then I'm your man to the end. If all this is just a showpiece to gain recruits then I'll leave and say nothing. You have my word for that.'

'I wish that it was a 'showpiece',' said the old man grimly. 'I wish that I hadn't discovered what I did but it's true enough and this equipment isn't just for effect.'

'Lorna said that the Arbitrators started all this, and she promised to prove what she said.' Dell slumped wearily onto the edge of the rumpled cot. His arm had begun to burn again, and tiredness filled his mouth with cotton and his eyes with grit. 'Have you any coffee?'

'Coffee?' The old man stared at the girl. 'Have we?'

'No. I couldn't get anything, the owners are beginning to dislike us. They

135

wouldn't even give me the scrapings from the dirty plates.'

'Here.' Dell pulled a few creased notes from his pocket. 'Send someone out for food and drink. I'm about all in.'

Lorna hesitated, then shrugged and took the money. 'He fought last night,' she explained to the old man. 'With knives, and he's cut a little. I'll get some medicine as well as food and drink. While I'm gone try and drum into that thick head of his what all this is about.'

She smiled at Dell, and the sound of her rapid footsteps died away down the sagging stairs. Carter coughed and busied himself a while with the scattered equipment.

'Have you ever wondered what caused the sudden breakdown of the old civilisation?' He pulled a stool opposite the cot and sat facing the middle-aged man. 'For as long as recorded history, way back to the first primitive tribes, men have always gathered in groups and obeyed the laws of such groups. The trend is a simple one, first the leader, elected by brute strength, then the king-priest concept, where an after-life system of reward and punishment helped to enforce actual law. Dictators, Presidents, Kings, all the various systems of government including Democracy and utter despotism have been tried, and all have sooner or later failed.'

'By internal corruption or decadence,' agreed Dell. 'What are you trying to say?'

'A simple thing. Man's strength lies in his ability to co-operate, to work together as a single unit. That fact has always been known, and ships, armies, industry and even entire nations have always stressed the necessity of the individual sublimating himself for the good of the whole. Each man had a duty to his fellows, and so it was that the Roman Empire conquered the ancient world, the totalitarian states almost conquered the modern world, and would have done so if the democratic powers hadn't adopted a similar system in order to win the war. Co-operation, Dell. Co-operation! The one thing we must have and the one thing we have lost!'

'Have we?' Dell shifted a little on the hard cot and tried to ignore the churning of his stomach. 'Even if we have what of it?'

'What of it!' The old man sighed and dragged his stool a little closer to the cot.

'Look at it this way, Dell. Just over thirty years ago we were armed and armoured as this planet had never been before. We had begun to develop space flight, and atomic power had been discovered and was being tamed. Admitted we were in two great camps, admitted that between us rose an iron curtain of mistrust and hates, but we were all men, Dell, and we had that thing in common.'

'I know all this,' snapped Dell impatiently. 'What are you telling me to convince me that the Arbitrators are enemies?'

'This!' Abruptly Carter spun a rheostat and the generator began to whine. A tiny screen flared with sudden light, a blue-green cathode emanation traced with a writing streak of brilliant red.

'Watch!' The old man made a careful adjustment and the red line danced and quivered, then steadied into a pulsing red band.

'That is controlled by the normal emanations emitted by the brain. Note that it is a steady pulsing, a smooth flow of electrical energy, minute, but even and predictable. Now watch.' He turned a switch and abruptly the red line writhed and knotted in ever-changing convulsions

'What is that?'

'That is the present brain pattern of electrical emission. The steady line is what we used to regard as normal, pre-arbitraton you might say, the recorded electronic flow as registered and recorded by various machines used in paraphysical research. That steady flow is a thing of the past, now the convoluted flow is normal and the even flow is non-existent.'

'Well?'

'Can't you see it even yet, Dell? Something caused that sudden change in the electrical brain-emission. Some outside force has disturbed the steady flow of energy through the brain cells, distorting and disturbing normal thought processes and making the world what it is today.'

'Perhaps, and then again, perhaps not.'

Dell sagged on the hard cot, and rested his throbbing head between his hands. His wounds burned as if they had been drawn with acid and an ugly darkness crept across the limits of his vision.

'A flickering line on a cathode screen, an assumption based on wishful thinking, a desire to shift blame and responsibility. Do you call that proof?'

'Yes.' Carter turned the switch, and the generator hummed into silence. 'Listen, Dell, and try to use what intelligence you may have. I told you that the Earth was armed and armoured as never before in all known history. We had weapons capable of turning a small planet into dust, rocket planes and guided missiles, we had everything, Dell, either to kill each other, or to kill any alien coming from outer space!'

'What!'

'Yes, Dell. If any alien had tried to conquer the Earth we would have been ready for them, nothing could have withstood the tremendous firepower of this planet. Our armies, air forces, military space agencies, and navies would have poured destruction into any invading fleet.'

'This is insanity!' Dell struggled upright on the narrow cot and tried to ignore the agony of his stiffening wounds. 'Now you are telling me that Earth has been invaded by aliens from outer space!'

'Yes, Dell. I am, and I wish that facts would prove me wrong, but they don't, Dell, they don't!'

'The Arbitrators?'

'Who else?' The old man sighed and wearily looked at his thin old hands. 'They came and no one noticed from where or how. One moment they didn't exist, and then they were in governmental positions, settling disputes, giving opinions, very friendly, very efficient and utterly remote. Have you ever seen an Arbitrator indulging in normal activities? No. They are sent for, they come, give their opinion and then return to the central offices, and, Dell, their opinions always favour the unrestricted use of free licence, anarchy, chaos!'

'You're right,' admitted Dell. He sat and remembered his own interview with the calmly smiling Arbitrator. The man had been logical, too logical, and he had decided on the side of pure freedom.

'Admitting that you're correct in what you say, yet how could a few men invade a planet? The Arbitrators are few in number, how could they be alien invaders, how would they conquer?'

'They aren't conquering, we are giving them Earth.' Carter rubbed his thin hand over his creased forehead and stared at the younger man. 'What arms have we now, Dell? Small arms yes, personal weapons, guns, pistols, rifles and a few machine weapons, but where are the rocket fleets, the navies, the armies? Gone, Dell, all gone!'

'How?'

'Isn't it obvious? What manufacturer makes war machinery now? Who would buy it? The factories make things which they can sell, pistols, turbine cars a few helicabs, but there isn't a factory in the world which turns out satellite-launchers, rocket planes, guided missiles, all the arms necessary to defend the planet.'

'Even so we have the old weapons, the

machines made thirty years ago, can't we use them?'

'Even if we could, and it takes a nation geared to a single-minded purpose to wage modern war, it wouldn't be enough. Most of the old machines have been melted down for scrap metal, the planes robbed of their scarce alloys, the atomic bombs dismantled for the power piles. No, Dell. We are sitting ducks, and they know it!'

Even then Dell couldn't quite believe the old man.

10

Lorna returned with medicine and food, a grey paste artificially flavoured, musty, yet highly nutritious and full of protein. She also brought energised coffee in cone-shaped thermocans, and as they ate the grey paste she thrust in the tops of the cans, swirling one between her hands as she waited for the chemical element to heat the liquid.

'Well, Carter. Did you convince him?'

'I'm not sure.' The old man swallowed and reached for a thermocan. 'I've done my best, but like most of them he can't believe in planetary invasion.'

'Why not?' Lorna stared at Dell and passed him a can of steaming coffee. 'Is it so incredible?'

'No,' he admitted, 'but why us? Why not land openly and be received as friends?'

'Friends!' She laughed without humour and her wide eyes were bitter. 'When man can't be friendly with man, how would an alien fare? You know what would have happened, guns and flame, the desire to smash and kill what couldn't be understood. It happened before, it would have happened again, and the results might have been too much for any planet to bear.'

'I don't see it that way,' protested Dell. 'We are intelligent people, even before the Change we had travelled into space and began to explore the solar system. We even discussed problematical meetings with alien races. We could have traded with them, shared the benefits of two civilisations, the Earth would have become a paradise.'

'You think so?' Lorna shook her head. 'Don't be blind, Dell, in a world where the colour of a man's skin or religion sets him apart, how could we ever have welcomed a race so different as an alien must be? No. I may be cynical but I know my own people, and I know just what would have happened to any trusting member of an alien race who would have landed here.'

'You talk as though you agreed with the Arbitrators!' Dell glared at her, feeling uncomfortable as he realised that she spoke the unpleasant truth.

'Then you believe what the old man told you?'

'Wait!' He smiled, and deliberately sank back on the hard cot. 'Was that what you were after? To make me annoyed and so take opposite sides to your argument?' He shook his head at her furious expression. 'I've still to discover how a handful of men could render an armed planet helpless. What I've heard explains nothing, proves nothing, and isn't that what you promised when you brought me here? Absolute proof. Well?'

'You're a blind, stupid fool!' Lorna glared at him her thin features tense and angry. 'Haven't you been told how it was done?' She turned to the old professor. 'Carter! Didn't you tell him?'

'Tell me what?' Dell shrugged and flung his empty thermocan into a corner. 'A babble of confused logic, sensible enough, but nowhere near to the absolute proof you promised me. I need better than a few extrapolations of what could have been natural cause. I want to see something beside a red line on a cathode screen, a line that could have been caused by anything. What I've heard has been interesting, but what you suggest needs more than a few wild guesses to make it undeniable fact.'

'So it's facts you want, undeniable facts!' She glared at him, then surprisingly laughed with pure merriment. 'Dell, why are you so hard to convince? Is it because secretly you know the truth but are afraid to admit it?'

He didn't answer, the woman was too near the truth for comfort and he hated to admit it. The old man wiped his lips with the back of one hand, peered into his empty thermocan, then with the irritation of age threw it into a corner. It rolled a little, coming to rest beside the one Dell had thrown previously, the metal making a faint sound in the silent room.

'Listen, Dell,' said the old man. 'I've shown you the two different patterns of brain emission, the one which we can term pre-arbitrator, and the one which is the present norm. Now something caused that alteration. Something external to us, an alien force, a radiation, perhaps a beam effect, but whatever it is it deranged the normal thought processes of the human mind and made the world what it is today.'

'Yes?' Despite himself Dell was interested in what the old man was saying.

'Now the derangement is an interesting one. To put it briefly it has by-passed the censor present in every human mind.' Carter stared at the younger man. 'I assume that you know what I'm talking about?'

'I know what the censor is, if that's what you mean.'

Dell wasn't annoyed. 'It is the something in the human mind which controls the flow of subconscious thought, restrains impulsive action and makes man different from animal. At various times it has had different names, soul, intuition, conscience, but whatever its name it made a man think twice before acting on emotional impulse.'

'You're not quite correct, but near

enough to suit our purpose.' Carter stared at the ranked instruments then at the intent face of the girl. She grinned at Dell.

'So you're not unintelligent, good. Carry on, Prof.'

'Very well. Now about thirty years ago something happened. Men grew tired of their jobs, and so they walked out. They grew angry with a man, and killed him. They wearied of taking orders, and so they refused to obey. It was a simple thing, men for the first time in recorded history did as they wanted to do and not as they felt they should. The result was chaos!'

'Yet you say the Arbitrators did all this?'

'Yes, Dell, they did. Earth was sprayed, is still being sprayed, with an alien form of radiation. I have separated and recorded it. A micro-wave pattern of incredible complexity flooding the Earth with a radiation which has distorted the normal thinking of every human being on the planet. Somehow it has cut out the censor, and now a man acts as he feels, on impulse, without conscience or regard to duty, utterly selfish and without shame.'

'One moment.' Dell stared at the old man, then at the silent figure of the woman. 'You say that every human has been so affected?'

'Yes.'

'Then what of us? What of the Antis? If they are without conscience how is it that they long for penalty-enforced law and order? Why of all men should they be different?'

'A good question,' admitted the old man. 'Will you answer it, Loma?'

'I joined the Antis because I saw both my parents shot down by a business rival. I saw my brother die in a senseless argument as to who had priority on a flight of stairs. I appealed to someone to avenge his murder, and help was offered — at a price. A price I couldn't and wouldn't pay. I've seen children starving in the streets, and once I saw a boy of ten kill his brother for a crust of bread. Isn't that answer enough?'

She paused, her wide eyes gleaming

with emotion and her slender figure quivering as she stared at Dell. He flushed and turned away.

'There is another reason,' said the old man. 'Not all brains are alike, there is a subtle differentiation, a variance from the norm so that while the alien radiation affects the majority of men, still there are a few who retain some shreds of what used to be called conscience. The Antis are recruited from such men.'

'I see.' Dell dragged his hand heavily across his eyes.

He felt shaken, as if his overstrained mind had finally accepted a truth too horrible to be accepted by any normal man. Earth invaded! The human race turned into beasts by some alien radiation, destroying themselves and the works of their fathers in senseless orgies of emotional catastrophe.

He stared sombrely at the old man.

'You said that an alien radiation is still being sprayed over the planet. How do you know that?'

'The final proof!' Carter smiled and rubbed his thin hands together in an odd washing motion. 'Once I had isolated the strange force it was a relatively simple matter to determine the point of maximum intensity, in other words, the origin. I searched for two years before I found it, and the discovery confirmed my suspicions.'

'Yes?'

'Look!'

The old man turned to his ranked instruments and threw several toggles. The generator whined again, and the screen of a small electroscope flared with sudden life.

Blue shone from it, blue and the fleecy white of drifting clouds. They slipped to one side, and as the range of the instrument increased, the blue of the sky turned dark and stars began to shine like little points of cold and distant fire. Carter adjusted several Vernier controls, then stood motionless beside the screen.

'Watch now,' he whispered. 'It will pass within five seconds.'

'What . . . ?' Dell half-turned to the old man, then jerked his eyes back to the screen. Something darted across the small panel, something bright and glistening, disc-shaped and flattened, something that caught the rays of the distant sun and reflected them in flashing glory.

A spaceship!

Dell stared, and stared, and stared, until his eyes burned and the tiny shape had long since flashed from the field of the small electroscope. Slowly he turned and stared at the old man.

'That was a spaceship,' he whispered. 'But that's impossible! All space programmes have been disbanded for decades!'

'Terrestrial programmes, yes,' Carter said. 'But that orbiting vessel did not originate from Earth.'

'It came from outer space?'

'Yes.' Carter snapped switches and the screen went dark. 'Now do you believe?'

Dell nodded. He was remembering all the old legends about what had once been termed 'UFOs.' Urgently he gripped the old man by one thin arm. 'Carter! What can we do?'

'Fight!'

Lorna stepped between them and gently removed Dell's grip. 'We haven't been idle, we of the Antis. We have always known that before we can even hope to restore law and order the aliens must die. That vessel is their single remaining ship, once destroyed the danger is averted and Earth can prepare for the next expedition.'

Dell was looking shocked — and puzzled. Carter attempted to answer his unspoken questions.

'We believe that when the aliens originally came, there were many vessels. To have remained undetected, their ships must have employed a cloaking device, perhaps some kind of force screen that rendered them invisible to the eye and radar.

'Once they had successfully infiltrated us, their fleet moved on, leaving this single vessel behind. It was only discovered by us a few years ago, when it suddenly became visible.'

'But why should it have done that?'

Carter shrugged. 'We don't know. Perhaps their cloaking device was using a great deal of power. Then, with the collapse of Earth's governments and space capability, they felt complacent enough to relax their defences in order to conserve it.'

'Can we fight?' Dell stared helplessly at the vibrant features of the woman. 'How?'

'We have the means,' she said grimly. 'That ship is a sitting target, we have plotted its orbit to within a fraction of a degree of arc. One guided missile, one atomic-headed war projectile, and we can send it crashing in a plume of flame and ash. One shot, Dell! One single shot and Earth is free again!'

'Can we do that?' He stared at her, hope swelling within him, then slumped as reaction and the cold truth of reality chilled his emotions. 'Lorna, how can we do that,' he said gently. 'We have no projectile, no atomic material for a warhead. What you plan is an idle dream.'

'No!' The old man glared at them, his thin face working with triumph. 'I told you that we have a backer, a businessman from another city. He has helped us, will help us more. We are waiting for him to bring the warhead, the rest of the projectile has been assembled and is ready for action. As soon as he comes we will fasten the warhead and fire the missile. It is self-guiding, and will detonate by means of a proximity fuse. We can't fail, Dell. We just can't fail!'

'Good.' He felt a surge of returning hope. 'What are the plans when the ship has been destroyed?'

'Kill the Arbitrators. Form an armed police force and draft regulations to be obeyed on pain of death. We will take over a few key cities, recruiting and expanding by geometrical procession as we advance. Within a few weeks we shall be masters of half the country, within a few months we shall dictate to the world, and peace will come again to Mankind.'

'I see.' Dell tried not to show his sudden doubts and suspicions. 'Who will form the police?'

'Naturally the Antis will form the nucleus, we will always remain in control and draft the regulations essential for the return of law and order. Naturally we expect some opposition but we shall be able to crush it with our united force.'

'Naturally,' said Dell drily. 'And I

suppose that your backer will be nominal head of the state?'

'Of course.'

'Did he make that a stipulation before he consented to aid the cause?'

'No.' Lorna stepped forward, her thin features distorted with anger. 'We asked him to head the work of reconstruction. He has aided the group for many years now. It would be unfair to deny him the position after he has done so much to help the cause.' She faced the younger man, her slender figure quivering as she read the cynicism in his eyes.

Neither of them heard a man enter the room.

11

Dell saw him first and stepped back into the shadows clustered around the generator. Carter saw him next and almost at the same time the woman became aware of the stranger. She turned, her hand lifting to her full lips, then gave a little cry of gladness and ran to the tall, slim figure.

'At last! Have you brought it with you?'

'Yes.' The man stared about the room. He was shrouded in a gaily coloured cloak, his face beneath the long visor of his stiffened cap, wreathed in shadows, but to Dell there seemed something familiar about the man. He kept well back, hugging the wall and watching with narrowed eyes.

'Where is it?' Carter was impatient and his thin body quivered in tune with his thin hands. 'The warhead, where is it?'

'I have it.' The man stared at Dell. 'Who is he?'

'One of us,' said the woman impatiently. 'Where is the warhead?'

'Never mind that now,' snapped the man. Deliberately he seated himself on the edge of the cot and as his cloak fell open Dell could see the twin butts of heavy pistols in their open holsters.

'Before I turn the warhead over to you, I want one thing made very clear. After the ship has been destroyed and the Arbitrators are all dead, I head the new state. Is that agreed?'

'Of course,' said the old man.

'Naturally,' said the woman.

'No,' said Dell.

He crossed the room with long strides and before the stranger could move had snaked the twin guns from their holsters.

'Take off that cap!'

'What . . . ' Angrily the man sprang to his feet. 'Give me back those guns!'

'Take off that cap,' repeated Dell grimly. 'Quick now!'

'Dell!' Lorna stepped towards him, her thin features convulsed with anger. 'What are you doing?'

'He's a spy, a dirty sneaking spy.'

Carter glared around him and stepped towards a rack of tools, his hand reaching for a heavy hammer.

'Hold it!' Dell gestured with one of his long-barrelled pistols. 'Stand back, Carter, or I'll smash your hand with a bullet. You too, Lorna.' He turned to the stranger. 'Are you going to remove that cap or do I take it from your dead body?'

Slowly the tall man removed the shielding cap of stiffened nylon.

'Well?'

'Bender!' Dell strode forward and thrust his face close to the pale features of his partner. 'Don't you know me, Bender? Can't you recognise your partner beneath the dirt and the brand you had tattooed on his forehead?'

'Dell.' Bender tried to step back and slumped onto the narrow cot.

'Yes, it's Dell, Bender. Surprised?'

'I looked for you, I had men search the city, but they couldn't discover where you had gone. What happened, Dell?'

'Don't you know?' Dell stared at his partner, his lips twisting as he recognised the craven fear filling the trembling man.

'You killed Madge, didn't you? Had me beaten up and branded, shipped to a different city where I'd be out of the way. You hoped that I'd die here, and I almost did, but here we are Bender, and you know what happens to anyone who breaks the Ethical Contract.'

Deliberately he lifted one of the pistols, aiming the small orifice directly between the other's eyes.

'I'm going to kill you, Bender. Kill you now!'

'No!' Lorna stepped between them, her thin features tense and desperate. 'You can't kill him, Dell. You can't!'

'Why not?'

'Because you've misjudged him. He couldn't have done what you accuse him of, I know he couldn't. He's our backer, Dell, the man who has helped us more than any other. The one man who can supply the warhead and enable us to destroy the alien vessel. You can't kill him! I won't let you!'

'Yes,' said Bender. He had recovered some of his normal assurance and he grinned at the strained face of his partner.

'That's right, Dell. Kill me and you lose the warhead, I'm the only man who knows where it is.'

'What of it?' Dell slowly tightened his finger around the trigger. 'What are the aliens to me? I swore to kill you, Bender, and I'm going to do it. Now!'

'Don't! Dell, don't do it!' Carter flung himself forward and gripped the younger man's arm. 'Please. You don't know what you are doing, I've worked for over thirty years to destroy the aliens, you can't kill the one man who can help us now. Think of it, Dell. One shot and the world is free again. Isn't that worth the life of one man? Perhaps you have suffered, but are you certain that he was the cause? Don't do anything you may live to regret, Dell. I'm sure that you are mistaken.'

'That's it.' Bender stared at his partner, the bright glisten of sweat shining on his forehead. 'I had nothing to do with it. Come back to the city with me, Dell. Together we can run things the way they should be run, Trust me, Dell. Trust me,'

Dell hesitated, the long-barrelled pistol

sagging in his hand. He stood thoughtfully biting at his lip as he stared at the
distorted face of his partner.

'Where is the warhead?'

'Safe enough. I can get it any time I
want.'

'Where is it?'

Bender smiled and fumbled in a
pocket. He withdrew a small box of
heavily ornamented plastic, and tapped
gently on the upper surface.

'That is my secret, Dell. When you have
returned my guns, promised not to harm
me, and have agreed to assist me in the
work still to be done, then I may tell you.'
He lifted the lid of his box. 'On the other
hand, perhaps I won't.'

He dipped his thumb and forefinger
within the box, smiled at his partner, and
lifted the pinch of cocaine to his nostrils.

Dell acted.

With the barrel of the pistol in his left
hand he smashed at the drug-loaded
hand of his partner. He dropped the
second gun and snatched the little box,
thrusting it deep within his pocket, and
stooping to regain the dropped weapon.

For a moment silence filled the room, then . . .

'Give me that box!'

Dell smiled and shook his head.

'Give it to me I say. Dell, if I don't get that box you'll never get the warhead. I'll see you in hell first.'

'Lock the door, Carter,' said Dell quietly. 'This may take a little time.'

'The box, Dell! Please!'

'Give him the box,' said Lorna. She stared at Dell, a frown creasing her high forehead. 'Why must you spoil everything like this? Surely you can see that you must have made a mistake about who injured you? He wouldn't do a thing like that to anyone, he has helped us more than you can ever guess. Give him the box now and let's get on with the important work.'

'This is important,' said Dell grimly. 'This is the man you intend making the head of the world. This is the new dictator, the iron ruler.' He thrust one of the pistols into his belt and retreated to the corner, sitting on the generator and resting his second gun on his knee.

'I know Bender better than any of you ever will. I know his rotten heart, his drug-crazed ambitions. Ruler of the world, that is what he wants to be, and you blind fools are helping him realise that ambition.'

'Someone has to be the head,' protested the woman. 'Why not the man who has helped liberate the planet?'

'Why not?' Dell twisted his lips in a bitter smile. 'I'm a businessman, and I look at things in a business-like way. How much has his help cost him? A few thousand credits at the most, some food, a few guns, a little ready money for equipment and the guided missile. The warhead is the most expensive item, and now I know why he had to get rid of me.'

Lorna frowned, staring at the grim figure sitting in the corner.

'How do you mean, Dell? Why did he have to get rid of you?'

'For money, for full control of our business, that's why.' Dell laughed as he saw the startled expression in her eyes. 'If you want to thank anyone for helping you, then thank me. It was my money he used to bribe you, my money he used to obtain the warhead. Don't you see it even now? He's been robbing me, robbing me blind for years now. When he needed the final sum for the warhead, he had to gain full control. With that he could flood the city with drugs, cash in on the artificially created demand, and with the money so raised he could buy enough atomic material to manufacture a warhead.'

'I see.' Lorna looked at the silent man sitting on the edge of the cot. 'What you say makes sense, but there's one thing you've forgotten.'

'Yes?'

'He didn't have to do what he did. Admitted he robbed you, but what of it? Isn't the end worth the means? A liberated world is surely worth a little harmless crime. What if he did rob you, would you have given us the money had we asked?'

'No.'

'Then where is the harm?' The woman smiled at the man on the bed. 'Don't worry, I can understand what made you act as you did.'

'Then tell him to give me back my box.' Bender half-rose from the bed, slumping down again at Dell's curt gesture. 'Make him give it back to me, Lorna. Make him!'

'Where is the warhead?' Dell asked the question without hope of a reply and he wasn't disappointed. He sighed a little as he stared at the woman's angry expression, and tried not to see the great tears of helpless frustration streaming down the old man's wasted features.

'You're convinced that he is genuine, aren't you Lorna? You are so certain that Bender is an idealist, of the same fanatical disposition as yourself. You are wrong. Bender is a self-seeker, and if ever you put him in full power you will live to curse the day.'

'I judge a man by what he does, not what his enemies tell me,' Lorna said coldly. 'I trust him.'

'Why?'

'For one simple reason. No matter how he got the money, yet he got it. No matter how much it meant to him, yet he spent it on a good cause. He bought a warhead, and that must have taken every credit he possessed. He is a ruined man now, and the least we can do is to see that he doesn't suffer by it.'

'You fool! You utter blind, incredible fool! What has he spent? The proceeds of selling something that wasn't his to start with, a small factory manufacturing cocaine. Sure he has spent all he had, but look what he stands to gain! A world to do with as he wills! You are going to make him the supreme dictator, make no mistake about that. At first maybe he will need you, but after he has recruited his own men, then you will be dispensed with as a nuisance. Study the old records of successful revolutions if you don't believe me, the pattern is as old as time.'

'We aren't quite fools,' she said coldly. 'We can take care of ourselves.'

'Can you?' Dell shrugged. 'I doubt it, but why let's argue. There is a simple test. You trust the man, then ask him for the warhead. If he is as genuine as you suppose then there is no reason why he shouldn't give it to you. That's why he bought it isn't it? For use against the aliens. Ask him to give it to you without bargaining, if he's an idealist he will give it to you even though he knew he was to die within the next ten seconds.'

Lorna hesitated, biting her soft lips and staring from one to the other of the men.

'Tell me,' she said softly. 'Where is the warhead?'

'Go to hell!'

She started back as if Bender had slapped her in the face, and her wide eyes filled with tears as she saw the crashing of her hopes and dreams. Dell laughed.

'That's no way to talk to a lady, Bender. These people trusted you, they have a guided missile here all ready to go. Why don't you tell them where the warhead is?'

'I want my box first. I want my guns and an assurance of supreme power. Give me my box, Dell, and I'll tell you where I've put the warhead.'

'No.'

'Please, Dell. Give me the box, or you'll regret it.'

'No.'

Desperately Bender turned to the woman.

'Make him give me the box, Lorna. I'll tell you then, I swear it, don't lose everything now for the sake of a glib-tongued fool with a gun in his hand.'

'Where is the warhead?'

'I can't tell you that, if I do he'll kill me, you know he will. Trust me, Lorna, give me the box and I swear that I'll tell you where it is. I want to get rid of the aliens as much as you do, you know that.'

'Where is the warhead?'

He gulped and slumped on the cot. Lorna stared down at him, her full lips twisting with disgust. Helplessly she glanced at Dell.

'What shall we do now?'

'We wait.' Dell lifted the little box, and smiled as he saw the craving in Bender's eyes.

'He is a drug addict, and this box contains his drug. He can't do without it, sooner or later he will tell us what we want to know. He will beg and plead for a sniff of cocaine, but eventually he must tell us how to get the warhead. He doesn't get the box until he does.'

'Are you sure, Dell?' Lorna bit her lips in indecision. 'So much depends on it.'

'I'm sure, Lorna,' be said quietly. 'You forget, I used to make the stuff.'

Tensely they sat down to wait.

12

It took two days.

Two days in which they watched the disintegration of a human mind, the collapse of dignity and the utter shedding of self-respect and self-determination.

Dell sat on the small generator in the corner, the pistol a leaden weight in his hand, the grit of utter fatigue rasping his eyes and his stomach churning with lack of sleep and disgust.

Twice he had fought the crazed man off. Three times he had jerked away from an uneasy doze just in time to save the precious box. More than once he had almost given in to Bender's desperate pleadings, and on the first day he had ordered the woman from the room.

Now it was over.

Bender sat and drooled, his mouth slack and his eyes glazed, looking like dull chips of brown glass against the deathly pallor of his strained features. He twitched with uncontrollable nervous reaction as his system craved the anodyne of the drug, and his fingers made little clawing motions as he stared unblinkingly at the man in the corner.

For him the Universe had contracted to the limits of the room, his existence to a single purpose. The box, and what it contained. He ran a dry tongue over cracked lips, and extended one hand.

'Gimme it,' he whimpered. 'I'm dying, gimme the box.'

'Where is the warhead?'

Dell whispered the question as he had whispered it a thousand times before Slowly he lifted his hand and snapped open the lid of the little box. He shook it, letting some of the contents rill in a fine white powder to the floor.

Bender whined like a dog and lunged forward, snarling with helpless rage as Dell thrust him back.

'The warhead,' he snapped sharply. 'Where is it?'

'Gimme the box and I'll tell you. One sniff and I'll tell you everything you want to know. One pinch and the warhead's yours.'

'Where is the warhead? Tell me now or I'll throw this stuff away. Tell me now or you'll never get what you want!'

Deliberately Dell raised his hand, and a thin trickle of white powder plumed softly to the gaping boards of the warped floor.

'Stop! Stop it, damn you!'

'Where is the warhead?'

Sweat glistened on the drug-crazed man's forehead. He gasped as though he had just run a dozen miles and his cheek twitched and jerked in a frenzy of nervous reaction.

'You'll give me the box if I tell?'

'Yes.'

'Central repository. Locker three-eighteen. Code word 'Liberty'.'

Dell sighed and nodded to the old man.

'You heard him. Take some men and hire a car. Have you money?'

Carter shook his bead.

'Here,' Dell emptied his pockets, then jerked a wallet from Bender's short jacket. 'Hurry. Better call in the group, we may not have much time.'

He listened to the old man run down

the stairs, calling breathless orders as he went. Lorna entered the room, staring wide-eyed at the whimpering thing on the bed, and biting her lips as she hastily glanced away.

'The box,' whined Bender. 'Gimme the box!'

Almost gently, Dell held out the little container.

Bender snatched it, dipped his thumb and forefinger deep into the contents, and stuffed the powder into his nostrils.

He grinned, snapped shut the lid of the box, and rolled slowly backwards on the narrow cot. Within seconds he was asleep, a thin smile curving his cruel mouth.

Lorna shuddered and clung to Dell.

'Not pretty is it?' He stared down at the unconscious figure of his partner. 'An ambitious man, too ambitious, and yet he is a slave to his own cravings.'

'He could be cured,' she said weakly.

'If he wanted to be cured,' agreed Dell. He stared again at the slumped figure on the bed. 'But who is going to cure him? Who is going to force him to give up the thing which is rotting his body and ruining his mind?'

'Why . . . ?' She hesitated, and Dell nodded.

'The only person who could cure him is just the one person who doesn't want the cure. Himself. No one else can make him do it, and that means that he will never be cured. Never. And what would the world be like with a hop-head sitting on the throne?'

He shrugged and turned away.

'You said that the rocket is here, does that mean it's within the building?'

'Yes. We built it from gathered parts, and it is here. Why?'

'Nothing.' He frowned as he stared at the equipment around the walls. 'Naturally you have a launching rack, firing controls, everything necessary to fire the missile?'

'We can manage.'

'That isn't answering my question. Have you?'

'Yes.'

'I see.' He stared down at her, trying to isolate the hidden emotion in her eyes. 'Show me.'

'Why?'

'Because I want to see it, that's why.' He laughed as he saw the doubt on her features. 'Don't you trust me?'

She stared at him, her wide eyes searching his tense features, then shrugged and moved towards the stairs.

'You may as well see it, there isn't anything you could do to stop it now.'

Together they descended the sagging stairs.

The missile rested in a crude launching rack within the building. A tapering thing of smooth metal plates, of flaring venturis, and an empty socket for the atomic warhead. Guiding fins surrounded it, and drums and cylinders of fuel lay stacked around. Dell stared at them, then at the hard-eyed men lounging around the rusty guides of the launching rack.

'Is it ready for firing?'

'Almost.'

'How do you mean, 'almost'? Is it ready or isn't it?'

'We still need the warhead,' she reminded acidly. He frowned.

'I know that, but has it been fuelled? Have the proximity fuses been set? Are the remote firing controls fixed and ready?' He stared at her sullen face, then turned with a curse at the lounging men.

'I might have guessed it! What are you all waiting for, the Arbitrators? Get this fuel in the tanks, get the missile ready for instant operation. Move!'

One of the men straightened and walked slowly towards him.

'Listen, you,' he growled. 'We do this our way, there's no sense in fuelling it up until we get the warhead.'

'Then fuel it now!' Dell stared at the man, then turned to Lorna. 'What is this? Don't you intend using the missile? When Carter returns with the warhead we should be all ready for him. Fuel the projectile. Fuel it now!'

She nodded, and snapped swift orders to the lounging men.

'Do as he says, fuel it up.'

'You know what this means, Lorna?' The man wiped the back of one hand across his mouth. 'If we pump the fuel into the tanks we'll have to fire the missile. The fuel is too unstable to mess about with. Wouldn't it be better to wait?'

'No. Fuel it up.'

The man shrugged, and barked at the lounging men. Rapidly they jerked into action, connecting flexible pipes to the drums of fuel and checking the pressure feed. Lorna smiled up at Dell, a strange expression in her eyes.

'Satisfied?'

'Yes. Why hadn't you loaded the missile before this?'

'The fuel isn't easy to get, and what the man said is true, it's too unstable to be handled safely. Once it's within the tanks we daren't touch it, gases build up and the danger of a premature explosion is too great.'

'Maybe, but it doesn't matter now. Unless Carter returns with the warhead the Antis are finished.'

'Finished? Why should you say that?'

He grinned and jerked his thumb in the direction of the upper room.

'You've lost your backer,' he said simply, then spun at the sound of an urgent shout.

It was Carter.

The old man was trembling with fear,

his thin body shook with it, and he glanced continuously over his shoulder. Dell gripped him by one thin arm, silencing the words bubbling from between his writhing lips, and jerked his head at the listening men.

'Later,' he snapped. 'Tell me later.' He turned to the assembled men. 'Quick now. Get the missile ready, load the warhead, fill the tanks. You know what has to be done. Do it!'

He pulled at the old man's arm, and together they climbed the stairs to the small instrument-cluttered room. Lorna joined them, shuddering a little as she glanced at the drugged figure of Bender, then looked at Dell.

'What's wrong?'

'I don't know.' He turned to the old man. 'What is it? Something has upset you. I could tell it from the way you acted. What was it?'

'The Arbitrators!' The old man raised a trembling hand to his mouth. 'The city is full of them! They seemed to be searching the city, we left the repository just as they entered it.'

'The Arbitrators?' Dell glanced at Lorna, then gripped the old man by the arm. 'Do you mean actual Arbitrators, or do you mean guards wearing the grey?'

'What's the difference?' Lorna moved beside the old man and glared at Dell. 'They're the same aren't they?'

'No. There aren't enough Arbitrators to search a city, what he saw were hired guards, they may not have been hired by the aliens at all.'

'Then why should they be here?'

'I don't know,' he admitted, and moved impatiently about the room. 'How much longer must we wait before the missile can be fired?'

'Some little while yet, we must wait for the orbiting vessel to enter the effective area of fire.'

'I see.' Thoughtfully Dell rubbed at his stubble-coated chin. 'The whole thing is automatic, I suppose?'

'Naturally. The missile has proximity fuses, set to detonate within effective range. They are both magnetic and radar. A large amount of metal will trip the trigger, or if the ship is non-magnetic its very mass will serve.'

Carter sighed and rubbed tiredly at his eyes. 'We must fire at the exact second of course. I have calculated the rate of ascent, the speed of the ship and its height. Once the firing stud is pressed the whole thing is out of our hands, beyond control, but we must make sure that we fire the missile at the exact moment.'

'You will take care of that, of course?'

'Yes.'

'Good.' Dell sighed and glanced at Lorna. 'Everything else has been taken care of, I suppose? The groups to kill the Arbitrators? The men to take over the key cities?'

'Yes.' She crossed the room and switched on the electroscone. For a moment she stood staring at the dark patch of empty sky mirrored on the tiny screen of the instrument, then irritably broke the contact.

'Plans have been made for all Antis to arm and assemble in Central City. They know what to do, and the detonation of the projectile will serve as a signal.'

'Then there is nothing we can do now?'

'Nothing.'

'He nodded and slumped down on the edge of the hard cot. He felt sick with fatigue, and resting his head between his hands tried to still the churning of his stomach. He longed for hot coffee, for warmth and good food, for rest and the comforts of his home. It had been a long time since he had known them, almost all of three days, or was it four?

Whatever it was it seemed an eternity.

His arm hurt and he wondered for the hundredth time whether or not he was doing the correct thing. Were the Arbitrators the monsters they seemed? Were the Antis the heroes they appeared? Could they reclaim the world to the dominance of men? Would he regret it if they did?

He didn't know, and somehow he didn't seem to care.

Time passed, slowly, relentlessly, drawing the hour of final decision ever nearer. A lamp flashed on one of the instrument panels, and Dell lifted his head as he heard Carter's thin reedy tones.

'Yes?'

A man's voice echoed softly through the room:

'Projectile loaded and ready to fire.'

Carter acknowledged the report, and he switched on the electroscope. He sat before the instrument panel, one thin finger poised over the firing control, his weak eyes staring with a disturbing savagery at the patch of almost black sky mirrored in the screen.

Bender stirred a little, muttering in his sleep, and Dell stared down at the man, an odd expression on his face.

'Carter!'

'Yes?'

'Would it be possible to trace the presence of radio-active elements?'

'Certainly. A geiger-counter would do it. Why?'

'The Arbitrators! You were right! They must have traced the warhead!' Swiftly he rose to his feet, and snapped quick orders at the pale-faced woman.

'Lorna! Warn the men, they must defend this building at all costs! Shoot on sight, we must hold them off as long as possible.'

He smiled grimly at the old man as the woman raced down the stairs.

'They must have traced the warhead, guessed what was happening and are trying to stop it. I . . . '

He paused, head slightly cocked, listening to the sounds below.

The thin spiteful sound of many shots!

13

Lorna burst into the room, her pale face tensed and her eyes deep pools of fear.

'Dell! The area is covered with guards. They are killing everything that moves. Dell! What can we do?'

'Steady,' he warned, and gripped her by one soft shoulder.

Bender muttered again, half-rising from the bed, then slumping back a foolish grin on his features.

Dell glowered down at the figure on the bed.

'If he had given us the warhead when he arrived this wouldn't have happened. That two-day wait gave them time to trace us, or perhaps someone told them what we intended to do.'

'A traitor? Impossible!'

'Is it?' He stared at her and smiled without humour as he lifted the twin weapons from his belt and checked the unfamiliar weapons.

'Dell! What are you doing?'

'Isn't it obvious? We need time, time for the orbiting station to enter the field of fire. We must get that time.' Gently he lifted her to one side and darted down the sagging stairs.

'Dell!'

He hesitated, then shrugged and carried on. Behind him the woman bit her lips until the blood rilled down her chin, then crossing the room, stared intently at he empty patch of sky mirrored in the tiny screen. Carter smiled understandingly up at her, resting his thin finger from where it hung poised over the firing control.

Neither of them noticed the man on the bed.

Dell hesitated at the foot of the stairs, wincing as something hummed through he air before him and exploded with a puff of incandescent gas against a wall. A man grinned at him from where he sprawled on the dirt of the floor, and Dell dived towards him, his guns ready in his hands.

'Where are they?'

'Everywhere.' The man spat and carefully squeezed the trigger of the old-fashioned pistol in his hand. He grunted, wiping the sweat from his forehead, and Dell recognised the branded doorkeeper.

'Many of them?'

'Like lice, we haven't got a chance.' He fired again, muttering a curse as the heavy pistol jerked his wrist with the recoil, and glanced enviously at Dell's modern weapons.

'Here.' Dell thrust one of the guns towards the man. 'You take it, I don't know much about them.'

'Thanks.' He glanced curiously at Dell. 'You point it, aim it, and squeeze the trigger. Try it.'

Dell nodded and peered through a crack in the wall.

Something moved in the alley outside, something like a grey spider, bent and crouching, legs pumping as it lunged for the cover of a heap of debris. Dell raised his pistol, squinted along the polished barrel, then squeezed the trigger. Dust plumed from a point just behind the scurrying shape, and he tried again.

Something smacked through the thin wood before him.

Something else shrilled through the air beside him, and the man at his side gave a peculiar choking grunt. Metal clattered, and turning, Dell saw the doorkeeper staring at him, a great blotch between his eyes.

It wasn't his brand.

Again Dell fired at something half-seen and too quick for a good aim. Outside the grey shapes seemed to increase, to be flooding towards the building, little spurts of fire stabbing from their hands. Around him men screamed and fired, cursed and died, sobbed and fell silent.

Somehow he knew that the battle was over.

He fired until his pistol was empty, then snatching up another gun, fired that too. He crawled away from the splintered wall, wriggling like a snake beneath a shrilling hail of humming death. The distance to the stairs seemed an eternity of time and effort, the journey up them a dragged-out nightmare. The firing had stopped, the screaming, the sobbing and the whispered curses. It grew very quiet, and in the silence a fresh sound throbbed and grew, roared and shrilled.

The sound of the missile!

And with it the scream of a woman.

Dell spun towards the room, forgetting the danger of shots and advancing guards. Lorna shrieked as she fought with a slender man with hot eyes burning against the whiteness of his snarling features. Carter lay slumped over the instrument panel, a thick rill of blood matting his thin white hair.

'Bender!'

'You . . . ' Bender flung the woman away from him and swayed a little as he stared at Dell. He smiled, a twitching of thin lips and a flash of white teeth. 'I've beat you, Dell,' he gloated. 'I've fired the missile, and I've fired it too soon. You've failed! Can you understand? Failed!' He laughed and the sound bubbled from his writhing lips like the eerie humour of the damned.

'I've beaten you, Dell, and now I'm going to kill you!'

Abruptly he lunged forward, hands outstretched and hooked fingers reaching for his partner's eyes.

Dell ducked. He crouched, folding his legs and bending his back. Bender lunged over him, hands clawing at the air, then with a surge of muscular effort Dell rose and catching Bender on his shoulder, threw him down the stairs.

He screamed once, then landed with a sickening snap of bone. He lay sprawled at the foot of the sagging stairs, his head wrenched unnaturally to one side. Staring down at him, Dell knew that he was dead.

Somehow he didn't care a bit.

Lorna came to him, creeping into the circle of his arms and stifling her sobs against the rough fabric of his tattered shirt. He stood there for what seemed a long time, staring at the tiny screen of the electroscope, watching the thin plume of the rocket missile as it climbed into the deep blue of the sky, climb, then fall, its warhead undetonated, its fuses still inactivated, falling to some lost landing in the depths of the ocean or the centre of a desert. Dell didn't care where it landed, all he knew was that they had tried — and failed.

He sighed, trying to comfort the sobbing woman, trying not to look at the old man with his smashed skull, trying not to think of the utter futility of it all. He turned, then stiffened, his muscles tensing in reflex to what he saw.

An Arbitrator smiled at them from the doorway.

Like all his kind he was tall and dressed entirely in grey. Grey blouse, grey trousers, grey eyes and grey hair. He smiled at them, and entered the room, glancing once at the slumped figure over the instruments, then staring at Dell.

'Why did you try to destroy our vessel?' He asked the question casually, as a man would ask about the weather. He smiled again at their silence.

'No. There have been no traitors in your group. Once we had the clue it was simple to extrapolate the rest. Naturally we traced the presence of a large amount of radio-active material, an elementary precaution against such a plan as yours. Tell me, why did you wish to destroy our vessel?'

'You — you admit it? You admit that you are alien?'

'Why not?' The Arbitrator smiled and looked around him. 'We are not of this planet, but neither are we alien in the true sense of the word. We are humanoid, even as you are, the only real difference between us is that we are mature while you are still adolescent. I use the terms sociologically you understand.'

'Why did you invade us?' Dell stared at the tall man, feeling the strange tranquillity always felt in the presence of an Arbitrator. He was curious, but not afraid, and his hate had dissolved as morning mist beneath the rising sun.

'Invade you?' The tall man shook his head. 'You know better than that.'

'Then why spray our planet with your radiant energy? Why derange our mental processes with forces from your orbiting vessel?'

'So you know about that?' The Arbitrator seemed pleased. 'Good. We had wondered how long it would take you to realise what had happened.'

'How can you stand there and admit

what you have done?' Lorna stepped forward her eyes gleaming with temper and disturbed emotion. 'Are you proud of the state of the world, the murdered men and women, the starving children? Why did you do this thing to us?'

'Why?' The Arbitrator looked down at her, and emotion left her face as if it had been wiped with a sponge.

'What have we done? We have saved your world. Saved it from atomic death, inevitable with the technology you possessed and the sociological structure of your civilisation. We aren't heartless invaders. We are members of a Galactic Federation, a union of worlds stretching among the stars. We discovered your world some fifty years ago, examined it — and found it rotten!'

'Rotten?' Dell swallowed and tried to imagine what the world must have been like some fifty years ago.

'Yes. Somewhere along the march to civilisation your race had taken a wrong turning. You had a high technology, but you used it as insane children would use it. You devoted the fruits of your science to build instruments of destruction, toys with which to kill and enslave others of your kind. When we discovered you, the world was hovering on the brink of racial suicide.'

He smiled a little, as an adult would smile at disobedient children.

'Naturally we couldn't allow that to happen.'

'So you sprayed us with your radiations,' mused Dell. 'Why?'

'Isn't it obvious? We gave men a gift, the gift of self-expression and self-determination. No man need do other than what he wishes. No man need obey the dictates of organised forces. Armies and governments have ceased to exist, and the race has time in which to breathe and regain its lost pride.'

'What of the starving children?' insisted Lorna. 'What of the drug addicts, the killers, the beggars? What of them?'

'Always in your history have there been children without food, men without the necessities of life, people who seek escape through drugs and fantasies. We did not create these things, you did, but they will all pass within two generations.'

'Are you certain of that?'

'I am.'

'Then you have had experience of this sort of thing before?'

'Yes.'

'I see.' Dell stared at the tall man trying to imagine what it must be like to be a member of a galactic civilisation. He failed, the concept was too vast for any normal man.

'So it is finished', he said tiredly. 'What is to become of us?'

'Not finished,' corrected the Arbitrator, 'the life of this planet has only just begun. Within two generations this race will have purged itself. Rid itself of all the recessive elements holding it back from true maturity. The killers will die before they can breed, the drug addicts, the insane, the weak. All will die, all will deserve to die, the weak, the unadaptable, the seekers after escape and protection. A race is as strong as the individual, no stronger. It is a law of nature, the only law we must recognise. Within two generations Earth will be populated by the best and strongest, and the strong are never cruel, never sadistic, never hurtful to their children.'

He turned towards the door, and Lorna cried out in sudden fear.

'What of us?'

Slowly the tall man turned and smiled.

'We are not ruthless. You have tried and failed and we recognise your courage, useless though it may have been. You are both fit and able, and there is a place in this world for all. Why not find that place?'

He smiled again, then was gone, and with him went the grey-clad guards.

It was over.

Dell drew a shuddering breath, and stared at the pale face of the woman before him.

'He was right,' he said slowly. 'Unless we can adapt ourselves to present conditions we deserve to die.' Automatically he touched his forehead. 'I can get rid of this. I have money in the city and now that Bender is dead I shall have full control of my business. A surgeon can remove this brand and we can live as people should live.'

'Can we, Dell?' Something in her voice drew him to her, and tilting her head he saw the glint of unshed tears.

'Have you doubts?' he whispered, then suddenly she was within his arms, and a great warmth for her flooded through him.

Gently he kissed her, then held her close again trying to still the quivering of her slender figure.

'They were right,' he whispered, and suddenly felt a great peace. 'The Arbitrators were right, this can be a wonderful world — now that we have their gift.'

Slowly he drew her from the room, towards the street outside, towards a new life.

He felt very happy.

THE END

We do hope that you have enjoyed reading this large print book.

Did you know that all of our titles are available for purchase?

We publish a wide range of high quality large print books including:
Romances, Mysteries, Classics General Fiction Non Fiction and Westerns

Special interest titles available in large print are:
The Little Oxford Dictionary Music Book, Song Book Hymn Book, Service Book

Also available from us courtesy of Oxford University Press:
Young Readers' Dictionary (large print edition) Young Readers' Thesaurus (large print edition)

For further information or a free brochure, please contact us at:
Ulverscroft Large Print Books Ltd., The Green, Bradgate Road, Anstey, Leicester, LE7 7FU, England. Tel: (00 44) **0116 236 4325 Fax:** (00 44) **0116 234 0205**

THE FROZEN LIMIT

John Russell Fearn

Defying the edict of the Medical Council, Dr. Robert Cranston, helped by Dr. Campbell, carries out an unauthorised medical experiment with a 'deep freeze' system of suspended animation. The volunteer is Claire Baxter, an attractive film stunt-girl. But when Claire undergoes deep freeze unconsciousness, the two doctors discover that they cannot restore the girl. She is barely alive. Despite every endeavour to revive the girl, nothing happens, and Cranston and Campbell find themselves charged with murder . . .

THE SECRET POLICEMAN

Rafe McGregor

When a superintendent in the Security Branch is murdered, top detective Jack Forrester is assigned to the case. Realising his new colleagues are keeping vital information from him, Jack Forrester sets out to catch the killer on his own. But Forrester soon becomes ensnared in a web of drug traffickers, Moslem vigilantes, and international terrorists. As he delves deeper into the superintendent's past, he realises he must make an arrest quickly — before he becomes the next police casualty . . .

THE SPACE-BORN

E. C. Tubb

Jay West was a killer — he had to be. No human kindness could swerve him from duty, because the ironclad law of the Space Ship was that no one — *No One* — ever must live past forty! But how could he fulfil his next assignment — the murder of his sweetheart's father? Yet, how could he *Not* do it? The old had to make way for the new generations. There was no air, no food, and no room for the old . . .